Arboreality

This is a work of fiction. All characters, organizations, and events portrayed in this novella are either products of the author's imagination or are reproduced as fiction.

Arboreality

Cover art by Rachel Lobbenberg
racheldesign.myportfolio.com

Edited by Selena Middleton

Published by Stelliform Press
Hamilton, Ontario, Canada
www.stelliform.press

Library and Archives Canada Cataloguing in Publication
Title: Arboreality / Rebecca Campbell.
Names: Campbell, Rebecca, 1975- author.
Identifiers: Canadiana (print) 20220242801 | Canadiana (ebook) 20220242836 | ISBN 9781777682323 (softcover) | ISBN 9781777682330 (ebook)
Classification: LCC PS8605.A5483 A73 2022 | DDC C813/.6—dc23

ONTARIO ARTS COUNCIL
CONSEIL DES ARTS DE L'ONTARIO

an Ontario government agency
un organisme du gouvernement de l'Ontario

For David Bourne

Arboreality

Rebecca Campbell

Stelliform Press ✸ Hamilton, Ontario

Special Collections

Jude had been teaching Engineering Communication and Design online for so long that the temporary virtual classroom seemed permanent. Every year or two someone in the department brought up in-person classes, but he wasn't surprised when the state of emergency extended another year, and they continued to wait for a return to normal that never came.

Though he rarely visited his office, he still needed books for his own work, which he sent out regularly to *Eighteenth-Century Speculum*. So he went in to campus on a wet Tuesday, passing darkened condo towers that had once been gilded and brilliant. When he was an undergrad, back in the 90s, the campus had been richly forested. Now the rhododendrons were dying while blackberries advanced from the forest's edge to the University Club.

He missed the familiar markers of his own early education. Drum circles. Atrocity exhibits. Chalk lines that purported to show the sea levels of 2100. Once he'd got absurdly high and fallen asleep in the middle of the quad with *Discipline and Punish* open on his chest, the day rising and falling around him. It was five before he crawled back to the bus loop, the book sunburned into his skin.

3

That earlier age was incredible to his students, even horrible: frivolity bought at a terrible cost, while they finished degrees in disaster management and experimental agriculture with placements in the swamplands of the former tundra, digging in to survive what the world would soon become, if they didn't first save it.

He was used to their increasingly angry questions, delivered via email or in chat: why should subject/verb agreement matter when I want to do quality control at a nuclear power plant? What does Ethos even mean if I'm installing photovoltaic arrays on the highway to Fort Mac or building a wind farm on Lake Eerie? Twenty years before, he had lectured them about communication standards in complex infrastructure projects, and told them that they would spend their entire careers writing, and that they should learn to do it well. But now, Jude had no answer that meant anything to them.

The light switch in the hallway didn't work. A poster on the bulletin board outside his office advertised a lecture that had taken place six years before. He had meant to attend. He had not.

Miraculously, the library was open. Inside, he began climbing the stairs to the stacks—

"—You!"

He turned and saw a woman silhouetted in the light from the entrance. Her hands were full: ice cream buckets, cleaning buckets, one with the old Canadian Tire logo.

"Go on," she said as she passed him. "Upstairs while there's time. It's breaking through in the southwest corner. We're going to lose all of Deleuze and Guattari."

Without speaking, he accepted the buckets she pushed into his hands and followed her. It had been a long time since he'd chatted with someone by accident, nodding as they traveled one way or the other, a promise of coffee later. He realized that he had not yet spoken, and asked, "You've been coming in every day?"

"More or less. What are you looking for?"

"Oh." He had to think, staring at the stack of ice cream buckets in his arms. "Volume seven of the Twickenham Pope."

It was good to chat, as people had done before the world grew so dire, and all contact had the quality of risk, and all the concatenated sorrows of the world seemed to drain away the pleasure of conversation from young people.

"Why are we carrying buckets?"

They reached the top floor where he saw a broken window someone had mended with garbage bags and cardboard. Berenice. That was her name. A PhD in information theory from some big American school. She led him to a corner where the ceiling was swollen and blackened.

"It's probably been collecting for weeks, but it only broke through today. I'll be emptying buckets all night."

The air smelled of stale paper, swollen with damp. Among the dull, earthy scents, though, a filament of freshness. Rain. He'd never smelled rain in here before.

"PR3620.F03," she called over her shoulder.

"Of course," he said, setting down the buckets and walking through the stacks to PR3620. His footsteps seemed so loud he walked carefully, as though he might disturb the students who no longer visited the sunny corner at the far end, with the bench on which one could— if one got there early enough — stretch out to nap. It was almost dry in the PR3600s. He remembered, suddenly, fighting with a girlfriend in that corner, shout-whispering insults at one another until some midterm stress-case shushed them. The Twickenham Pope had survived, rippled with damp. The brief illusion of normalcy vanished. He might turn a corner and find ducks drifting in a study carrel, or a waterfall flowing down the emergency stairs.

Downstairs, Berenice was sitting at a desk near the window, chaotic with paper, her laptop glowing.

"Don't they know?" he said, putting down the books.

"I've sent memoranda, but there's no money, and I'm not even sure there's anyone to answer them. I imagine they're building up somewhere, a giant inbox full of unread messages detailing the total collapse of McPherson library."

"It's just you, then?"

"I have a few student volunteers. Some faculty come in. Do you remember Dr. Cho? The Miltonist? He was the one who snaked the drains in the basement during that really heavy rain in September. The poor man was soaked through for days, but he managed it. I couldn't have done it."

He sat on the dusty plastic chair beside her desk. "What are we going to do?" He felt helpless asking, and heard the mild accusation in his voice, unwarranted.

She spoke as though prepared for the question, and answered painfully, truthfully: "It's not going to survive as a collection. There are retired faculty who will help. And students still in town. I've been working on a list. We'll need records, and a plan for distributing copies in a number of places. We should assume a great deal of loss."

As though he didn't grasp what she said, he went on, "I could help you with some of the leaks, we could go up through the ceiling —"

"— but there's no saving the building." She said this surprisingly gently. "Not if we're thinking ahead. And we should think farther ahead than next semester, or next year. Even if the satellites work, connectivity will only get spottier — think about what happened after the last landslide in the interior. We're going to need books again, for a while at least. Maybe forever. But we can't if they're all turned to mush and locked away on campus."

"What do we save? Beyond Pope, obviously."

"Pope. And animal husbandry. Geography. Geology. How to extract teeth. How to run a homestead." This time she laughed. "A *homestead*."

Jude felt cold, but it was not a new chill: it had been with him for years now. It crept under his skin as he understood that the world he had been made for was disintegrating around

6

him. He'd be left behind with it, dreaming of coffee shops and WiFi while all the children adapted to a new forest even now overtaking the abandoned condominiums at the margins of the city.

During the first winter of their conspiracy, Jude felt both elation and exhaustion. Despite Dr. Cho's ingenuity, they lost the basement in the April rains, and locked the doors permanently on the gallery, the old compact shelving, and the microfiche.

The library was crumbling and the trans-mountain connections to exchanges in Alberta were increasingly unreliable with each flood and landslide. But then he thought of how it felt to read *Kindred* and *The Fleece* and a thousand other books, and his heart was tender and brilliant with hope. He considered the undigitized audiotapes in the archive downtown, at sea-level, all those voices, and wondered what would happen to them, imagined those basement rooms below the old museum flooding, the weeping concrete walls, the long tables, and white gloves, and tiny pencils, the coat-check room, all ankle deep in water, then knee deep, and the watery darkness glowing, slightly, with some as-yet-unevolved phytoplankton that thrived on dissolved concrete.

Twice a week, Jude walked the stacks with lists he'd made on the backs of old essays. For the first time in years he felt rich, profligate, pulling books from the shelves, and packing them up to find their way out into the world.

The tide pool holds 2.35 liters of salt water, cupped in a massive deposit of quartz diorite on the western shore of Saanich inlet. The pool has been here since the morning of 26 January 1700, when the last megathrust earthquake shook it into place. The 2.35 liters are refreshed every twelve hours

and twenty-four minutes by a new tide spilling over its lower, southeast-facing lip. In three centuries, it has shared the inlet with ocean gardens full of mussels, middens, beach parties, clear cut logging and industrial fishing, ocean acidification, Jet Skis, and salmon runs. In that time, life in the pool has presided — from a distance — over the fashion for pompadours on men and scandalous two-piece bathing suits on women. It has held sea snails, barnacles, limpets, and hermit crabs who feed on the rich biofilm that coats its walls.

This day in July is so still the water hardly moves, and the air seems to hang from the branches of arbutus trees above the little pool. At two in the afternoon, the temperature reaches 31°C. Granite doesn't mind, of course, but the evaporating water leaves a thin salt-crush on the edges of the pool. For a week, every consecutive afternoon is hotter than the one before. 32. 35. People in the Cowichan Valley rise early to soak their curtains before they withdraw into the darkness. 37. The woods are dry. The deer so still they seem already heat-stroked. The rabbits have all disappeared.

From Tacoma to Port Hardy, high pressure drives the cloud cover away, further compresses and heats the atmosphere. 39. 42.

To people standing on concrete in the treeless neighborhoods, the air feels like insulating glass, thick and darkly gold. The blue sky is hot to the glance.

43. 46. In Victoria, a poor girl renting a crooked room dreams of rain. The grid flickers and fails one night. The beaches are full of strangers, sleeping side by side in the darkness. Twelve children die on the first night, and forty-three terminally ill people in a nursing home. Those families who can afford it flee to an air-conditioned movie theater out-side of town that's showing director's cuts of The Lord of the Rings, *and children fall asleep across their parents' laps, sticky with treats, begging to go home to bed.*

In the early mornings the water and the rocks around it are cool. The barnacles are attached by their heads to the ground, using the cement they excrete to attach themselves and build their outer shells. By noon the water is hot to the touch, 51°C, and in the long, still afternoon that follows, proteins in the barnacles' bodies denature. Cells can no longer undertake the necessary functions of life. At low tide, the whole beach smells of rot, the open mouths of mussels.

In Victoria, an eighty-five-year-old woman in an apartment on Fort Street with south-facing windows sees the sunrise and thinks, this day will be unendurable. She is already dehydrated, her blood thickening in her body. It is 47 degrees in her tiny, airless room. She has sprayed the curtains down with warm tap water. She sits near the window, her legs too swollen to walk, and thinks of a day in 1945, when she was small, and standing in a tide pool in the rock that underlies Saanich Inlet. It is 48 degrees in her apartment. She thinks of water, of climbing onto barnacled rocks. 49 degrees. It is 50 degrees. She should be careful not to cut herself, but the water around her foot is already stained red. In her brain the thickened blood clots. She's bleeding. She's bleeding.

Rainy days when the scent of water rose from the basement. Stifling days when climbing the stairs was like ascending to hell. Smoke-filled days and dark days when the grid flickered and he wondered if it would ever stabilize. On all these days, Jude collected books and carried them out of the library, where Berenice's old car waited, and together they delivered them to sympathetic homes all over the city.

Soil science. Animal husbandry. First aid. Diseases of the chicken, duck, and pig. *Love and Rockets.* Diseases of the potato and the principles of distilling. The dangers of methanol.

Natural dyes. *The Faerie Queene*. Optics. The signs of stroke. Diabetes. The bloody history of empire in North America. The immune system. Beneficial molds. Dangerous molds. The history of the kayak. The lost Megafauna of North America.

Coast Salish architecture and principles of construction.

But there were far more books than there were places to safely send them, now that the fires had overtaken Sooke, and the Great Desettlement of Vancouver Island had begun. Each year Jude grew more selective:

Beethoven's *Kreutzer Sonata* or "Where Does That River Run?" or "Don't Get Around Much Anymore" or "Gymnopédie No 1" or *Company*?

An oral history of west coast punk or a decent survey of the Second World War?

The Seven Lamps of Architecture or *The Souls of Black Folk*?

The Bhagavad Gita or *Journey Into the West* or *War and Peace*?

Crystal radio sets. *Hydriotaphia, Urn Burial, or, a Discourse of the Sepulchral Urns lately found in Norfolk*. Morse code. The lymphatic system. *Bodies that Matter*.

A biography of de Sarasate. The history of the violin and principles of its construction. Joinery. Wagoya.

The construction of hammers, both metal and stone.

He wondered what he had denied the future: Some fact they would need in twenty years: how to mend a photovoltaic plate, or set a leg or cure croup or make a smoker.

He was tired, cold in the damp sunless hall, but on this day in January, several years after he and Berenice had begun dismantling the collection, he stopped in at SB469-476.4. Landscape architecture. From the shelf, he pulled a book full of diagrams and photographs of trees: coppicing and inoscula-tion, pleached Italian hedges and espaliered peaches in a

Provençal gardens, tanzlinden in German villages and baubotanik towers in Denmark. The living root bridges of Meghalaya. Bleachers of rubber fig roots, from which young men craned their necks to watch cricket matches. Furniture not made of wood, but grown from the branches of living trees. He could imagine, suddenly, a future world in which these were ordinary, lives lived in the branches and among the leaves.

The book was too heavy — as Berenice had put it — to carry with you if you were fleeing a plague or a flood. But nevertheless he packed it in a box bound for a friend in the Cowichan Valley, who had volunteered a whole room to the cause.

He'd known Berenice for decades, her rigor and advocacy and bone-dry humor. Daily, now, he was relieved to know she was still in town instead of moving east or north to the huge mining towns, where people could gather at cafes in the black-fly summers and watch the smoke rise above the wildfires. She could have gone. Her oldest son was a mining engineer. There'd be grandchildren. But Berenice was still here with her ironic smile, reserved for snotty grad students and over-reaching administrators.

"Did you hear," Berenice told him when they met, "U of T scooped the first quarto from the legislature library? I'm not surprised. That's U of T all over."

He laughed. "Maybe we can be greedy, too. What do you want?"

They were on the third floor, white-gloved in the flickering light of the three remaining fluorescent tubes in the ceiling.

"I shouldn't."

It hurt to hear that. "I thought it should stay nearby. We'll want to re-assemble it when —" that stopped him. He tried again: "It should probably go out to Cowichan as well."

He picked up a nineteenth-century chart of the Salish sea, one of many they had taken before the basement flooded, left behind when U of T cleaned out Special Collections.

"You should take it," Berenice said.

"I have too much already. If my house goes, we'll lose most of the eighteenth century."

"But there should be some reward, shouldn't there? Take the charts."

That night the power failed and he looked at the old charts and remembered the shape of the islands as they had once been, from Desolation Sound to Oak Harbour. Now the mouth of the Fraser gaped wider across Delta, and Lulu Island had begun to drop under the water. Saltchuck rushing northeast to overtake the old coastline of False Creek. The museum of Anthropology at UBC sliding down the sand cliffs to Wreck Beach. He traced the old parameters of the world, as he had known it, as a kid, as a young man, and touched the inter-section in Kitsilano he'd loved on warm evenings. His apartment on Fraser Street, in the attic of a rotting house full of squirrels. BuTo seminar rooms. These ghostly and irrelevant maps, he thought, are they even worth preserving? The old folds, the wear marks, the annotations in a fine inky hand.

He rolled them up then set them in his old backpack, open at the top like a quiver of arrows.

Dr. Tremblay had taught him geography. He had been a kind man. He now lived with his grandchildren on the shoul-der of Mount Newton, above the low-lying suburbs of the Saanich peninsula. Jude had plugged the address into one of those apps that showed you future coastlines after one meter, or ten, and it was safer than many places in Victoria.

The day was dusty and quiet. That was, he thought, an unexpected benefit of this slow apocalypse, no more drum cir-cles or movie sets to avoid while crossing campus. He had come to enjoy the permanent Sunday-afternoon silence that now occupied the whole city. He stowed the maps in his backpack and set off slowly into the smoky air. It took him three hours to get to the gate with the golden arbutus, and the driveway was so steep he got off his bike and walked.

"I've never seen golden arbutus," Jude said at the front door. Tremblay did not invite him inside, but sat with him as he drank a glass of water on the porch. Somewhere, the grandchildren were playing.

"I'm not sure where it came from. Some mutation, or maybe one of the genetic modification projects Guillaume did in forestry. He brought them home sometimes."

"He's —"

"— Three years now. The most recent plague."

"I'm sorry to hear that."

"You're teaching from home, I imagine? Since the latest?"

"I am."

"What are the plans to reopen?"

It wasn't a question anyone asked anymore. He said, "Someone suggested it would end this year, but that doesn't seem likely."

The sky turned purple in the west. Smoke stained the last sunlight a rich, dark amber. Together, they looked down the hillside through drying cedar trees and the dead branches of drought-stressed arbutus.

"Do you know," Dr. Tremblay said, "that an arbutus tree saved the Saanich people during the flood?"

"Flood — last year? When Elk Lake —"

"— No. The great flood." Jude listened with pleasure, like it was a digression on Salish mythic hydrology in some first year geography lecture. "Anyway — the waters were rising and had covered the village, so they got into their canoes and set off for the only peak still visible — Mount Newton — right here. By the time they reached it, the only thing above the water was an arbutus tree. That's how they didn't lose one another. They tied their canoes to a tree at the top of this mountain until the waters abated."

"One of these?" Jude asked, looking at the golden trunk below him.

"The old kind, there. *Arbutus menziesis*. Not the new kind, whatever that is."

Jude did not mention the obvious lesson: that this arbutus was dying. He let the thought pass, and asked, "Could I trouble you for another glass of water?"

"It's a beautiful tree," Tremblay said. "Excellent firewood, though not much use in woodworking."

Jude swallowed drily. Perhaps Tremblay hadn't heard his question. He lifted the old charts from his backpack and said, "Berenice and I thought you should have these."

"Berenice? Who's that?"

"Dr. Alexiou."

"I don't know an Alexiou."

"McPherson library is falling apart. We're trying to save what we can and we thought of you —"

"— U of T removed everything of value for the duration."

"Not everything. There's a lot still there, and the roof won't last many more years. We decided to save what we could."

As Jude unrolled one of the charts, Tremblay seemed suddenly energized, as he had once been at the head of lecture halls and conference rooms.

"This is — you should have been more careful, Jude. What were you thinking? A bicycle." Tremblay clucked, then carefully turned the pages, using his sleeve to protect them from his fingers. "You took these? I didn't think you were —"

Jude looked longingly at the empty glass while Tremblay harangued him. He was surprised by his own exhausted patience with the old man's rage. Tremblay belonged to those earlier years, a campus that was green and full of students, voluble conversations at conferences, long dinners at twilit patios downtown. All his work had been undertaken in hope, trusting that the institution would still exist to preserve his books: *The Hauntological Coast; Psychogeography of a Canadian Empire.* Those books had been a pleasure to read, generously illustrated and printed on heavy paper. He'd included them in a box he'd sent up island, with books about animal husbandry and plate tectonics.

Tremblay was boiling now: "I'll call them, Jude. I'll tell them what you've stolen. What did you think I'd do when you brought me this?"

He thought of Berenice under the steady drip of rain through the holes in the roof and Dr. Cho soaked to the skin, clearing the drains. He nodded. "If you like. More than anything, I hope you'll take care of them until someone can come for them."

Jude coasted down the winding driveway among the dying cedar and arbutus. Before he turned onto Mount Newton Crossroad, he stopped and wondered if he could get water at one of the other houses, then dismissed the thought. That was when he saw another golden-leafed arbutus, glowing richly as the sun set. The tree was both familiar — its long, searching trunks, its smooth bark — and alien in its color, which shone in the dying light, as though it had gathered the sunset to its skin, and shed it again as evening came on. A new tree for a new world, he thought, then pedaled slowly home.

Controlled Burn

In July, Bernard started digging where the grass had already died after the watering ban. When the season changed, he'd plant closely: Oregon grape, both tall and dwarf varieties, wood roses and salmonberries in the shade, salal. In the middle of his suburban front yard, he would add a Garry oak sapling —

"— Doing some gardening?"

Jim Delacourt from across the street. He'd finished cutting his lawn.

"Yup."

Jim waited.

"How's Jen?" The silence stretched thinner. "Bernie?"

Bernard opened his mouth, closed it. Who wanted to talk about that?

"Okay. Well. I'll let you get to it."

Bernard drove the shovel further into the grass, turning over another clod and revealing what lay beneath them all, the dense clay of the hillside, like a cracked rock in this weather. Another shovel, another turn, and he felt something inside him shift. Maybe the bursitis in his right shoulder acting up. Maybe his heart.

Arboreality

Jim hauled water in from work to keep his begonias and impatiens brilliant in the dry heat, even when the air was full of ash and the evening sky a dull sepia. On Saturdays he cut the lawn with a riding mower, first parallel with the curb, then at a precise 45-degree angle from corner to corner. He edged it and sprayed for weeds, and then — Bernard had seen this, he was sure — he stopped for a moment before he pulled the mower into the garage, and was satisfied, a dream fulfilled briefly in the late afternoon, despite the black grit floating down the hillside and dulling the shine on his cars.

Bernard watched him in horror and wonder, entranced by his precision and surprised by the pleasure they both took in the lawn each summer, its richness, its softness underfoot. It looked like someone's vision of a lawn. It looked like a post-card from a dream-town that never existed: *Greetings From Cowichan!*

When she was little, his daughter Octavia had loved Jim's lawn. He could still see her running across it and into the back-yard, where she'd screamed on the trampoline, barefoot and tangle-haired, a wild girl struggling to keep up with Jim's daughter Caroline. Where had Caroline gone? Toronto, maybe. Or one of the palladium mines on James Bay?

Bernard's own lawn was a mess — dead clay on the corner he always cut when he pulled into the driveway, and a flurry of dandelion heads nodding above the grass.

"The problem" — this is what the bylaws officer told him on the second visit — "is that there are a lot of rules still on the books about grass height, especially for front yards."

"It's not grass."

"I understand, but there are still bylaws. Either you clean it up or we have to. And then we have to bill you. No one wants that."

"Okay, but there isn't an HOA."

"There's fireweed growing in there now. And it looks like you're losing a lot of grass to moss under the cedar. Dandelions, too."

"Yup."

"I wish I could help you."

"Well. Do what you have to do."

Frustrated in the early summer heat, the young man left, tapping notes into his phone as he ducked between the Oregon grape and the fireweed. In its third year, Bernard's scraggly garden had begun to look like the forest it would one day become. There were two oak trees in the back now, rising above the edibles: camas, wild ginger, stinging nettle. He was raising a Pacific crabapple to put out front, too, when the weather cooled down in November.

Across the street, Jim spread peat from his mower. The guttering chug of the engine and the scent of diesel were both things Bernard loved, though they felt like relicts. From atop his mower, Jim watched as his neighbor cut up more dry turf and put in trillium and kinnikinnick and hairy manzanita. The path that wound to his front door was so narrow his hands brushed spirea on either side. It had overtaken the fireweed, as was right, in the progression of species from suburban front yard to — something new.

Then one morning he woke up to find his front walk had been edged where the moss spilled over onto the concrete. A week later, the ragged yarrow he'd planted along the curb was dying, its leaves turning the distinctive orange-brown you saw in ditches cleared with brand-name glyphosate. After the yarrow died, the goldenrod followed, then the fireweed.

Not entirely surprised, he collected the dead plants and started over again.

Arboreality

Bernard stood on his front step watching Michelle and Chris prepare to leave. His neighbors were two surprisingly old people, their kids long gone, now packing up a small car on their way to who knew what — some government-built complex in London, Ontario, half-buried in the ground to moderate temperature in the blazing summers.

"47°C in that last heatwave," he said to Michelle, as they carried boxes out of the house.

"You should come, too. Or maybe Calgary? Isn't Octavia in Calgary?"

"Whitehorse, I think. She doesn't want an old dude hanging around."

"You could stay with us for a while. Jen would —"

Silence descended. Michelle seemed to reconsider the book in her hand. She had always been pretty, Bernard reflected — now, and back when she first moved in, when the yards were flat and raw and covered in farmed turf. When the trees were all frail, spindly things. Impossible — he had thought — that they would ever reach above the houses' roofs or offer shade on July afternoons. The kids all running together in the evenings, blowing bubbles that drifted above the rooftops. Halloween candy and Easter egg hunts. Now —

"What can I do?" He picked up the box taped shut, labeled "kitchen" and carried it to the trailer.

"I don't know. Goddamnit, we paid off the mortgage ten years ago, so we're not upside down. But — Yeah. Work or Mincome. I don't know. Chris made up his mind last year. And I get it. I don't want to watch another town burn after what happened in Sooke. "

She picked up another book. Looked at it. Threw it into the discard heap on the floor. "You could get set up while you still have a few years of work left in you."

"47 degrees. And they don't have the water."

19

"We'll leave you the keys, okay? If you want to plant your goddamn camas go ahead. And there's a bunch of *Rolling Stones* from the 90s in the basement. There's an interview with Salt-N-Pepa I've been meaning to re-read."

"When you come back."

"Sure. When we come back. I'll grab it then."

Unspoken: when the world is changed again for the better, and we can rediscover the places we love like they'd been there all along, the cities brilliant and full of people, the 7-Eleven stocked with cold drinks, your parents waiting at the door, clean sheets on your childhood bed.

Brief, tight hugs and goodbyes and it all felt absolute, even if he'd see their pictures on his phone, and Michelle would text him links to particularly enraging news stories. She might as well be on one of those Mars missions that still took off from Kazakhstan, the ones you heard about, but which seemed to go silent, no selfies returned from the biospheres they built in the lava tubes of Arsia Mons.

After Michelle and Chris left, the block was startlingly quiet. On moonlit nights, he walked down through the streets toward the main road, and thought he could see the heat-strained Douglas firs lean further into the temporary clearing of their cul-de-sac. Why hold them back? he asked himself. Why?

No one bought Michelle and Chris's house. Jim fell. His son visited for a week, then left again, and in his place a homecare nurse arrived morning and night — private, Bernard guessed, since regional health had cut most mobile services by then. He went over to check on Jim once or twice a day, and pulled dandelions from the lawn in the evening. A month later, Jim fell again.

"You'll be happy to see me go." He said it without apology, a fact.

"No." Bernard wasn't exactly lying. "Where are you going?"

"Mainland. Interior."

"That's a long way."

"They have a pool. There's an extra room. Mountain air."

Jim coughed wetly, a slug-trail of mucus down his chin. Behind him, boxes emerging from the house and disappearing into his son's SUV. Bernard couldn't remember the kid's name. Much older than Octavia, tearing around on his bike when she was a toddler. So many expensive toys. The car his parents bought when he turned eighteen. He'd followed pipeline work into the mountains. Something in management.

"Did you poison my goldenrod?"

"He should have been out of here years ago," a woman's voice from inside. "It's ridiculous."

"The seeds get everywhere. Looks like rags when the flowers die. And you never cut them back in winter."

Bernard nodded. "You're supposed to leave them standing for the birds. What about the camas?"

"I like camas. And those oak trees. I like oak trees." He coughed again. "You'll be happy to see me go."

"What's going to happen to the house?"

Jim shrugged. "Keep an eye on it for me. Water the grass. You can have whatever's in the shed. Probably most of what's in the house, too. Canned food in the basement. Tuna. She doesn't like tuna."

In the house, Jim's daughter-in-law left things behind: the books and the pool table. The mower, the Christmas lights, the model cars and framed Canucks jersey, the giant screen TV with all the speakers.

"You should go." Jim said. "You're young enough to start over."

Bernard snorted. "Young," he said.

Jim didn't laugh. "Why not?"

21

Behind them, the car slowly filled with the smallest number of objects an old man would need in a new life in his son's spare room. "Octavia wouldn't know where I am," Bernard said, finally.

Jim nodded and said nothing, then put his hand on Bernard's shoulder, the most affection they'd shown one another in thirty years.

Garry oak savannas are successional landscapes. They are a temporary response to disturbance by fire, existing between ash and the mature Douglas fir forests that dominate that coast from northern California to Quadra Island. When these savannas persist for more than a few decades, they are the product of human intervention. Industrial logging and sub-urban sprawl both prevent fires instead of using them strategically, and Garry oak savannas at the northern edge of the range disappeared quickly into the Douglas fir. A hand-ful remained after resettlement: in the Cowichan Valley, and one on the banks of the Fraser River.

Of course, even the trunks of oak trees will burn in a violent wildfire, but their roots survive, sending up new shoots the following spring. Camas will grow up through the burnt grasses. The Douglas fir seedlings die, and the deep forest recedes temporarily, leaving this open, sunny land, maybe on a south-facing hillside, above the water.

Nineteenth-century settlers thought the Salish coast's forest was green and innocent, stretching away from them like possibility. What they did not recognize were sea gardens full of cultivated mussels or forest gardens rich with crabapples, or oak savannas. What they encountered was a landscape of fire.

Arboreality

Bernard avoided Jim's house for months, until a heavy November downpour flooded the street and he saw a broken window. There was glass and rainwater all over the floor in front of the TV. His first impulse was to cover the window, but he stopped himself and instead searched the kitchen and basement. He found tuna and a half-bag of bird seed. He found weed killer and rat poison and a collection of terracotta pots. Outside again, he said something like a prayer and doused the surviving plants of Jim's perennial border — the periwinkle, the English ivy, the lavender — with glyphosate.

That winter, he expanded his new forest into the Ervine's yard next door, putting in another oak tree, two more apples. Each season he further blurred the property lines, and with them the lineaments of his old life — the yard where Octavia had played, where he and Jen had hosted barbecues — gave way to this eager wild, which had been waiting for forest fires and the settler exodus so it could recover the world in fireweed.

More people left after each fire season. They ended up in Yellowknife where there was work in the softening permafrost, fighting fires and working on experimental farms, with plants engineered for the bogs and a short, brilliant growing season. You heard about jobs on Great Slave Lake, or mining palladium in Moosonee. He held their keys, but none of them came back, and it reminded him of stories he'd heard as a kid about Montana and southern Saskatchewan, the husks of dust-bowl houses still standing after someone turned the lock in 1933 and left forever.

Without neighbors, the cul-de-sac was now entirely populated by ghosts. Octavia as a little girl, scrambling across the drainage ditch at the bottom of the subdivision, through a belt of woodland to the farms beyond, where blackberries grew along the fenceline. On a Saturday afternoon in early

September, she found her way to the garage where he was sharpening the blade of the lawnmower. She offered up a basket she'd made from a maple leaf, feeding the stem through each leaf point in turn, before filling it with fruit. Her lips purple and her fingernails blackened.

"Thanks, Tavia," he said, and together they sat on old aluminum lawn chairs that had belonged to his childhood and ate.

"Do you like them?" she asked.

"They are the best blackberries I have ever tasted."

He wasn't lying.

"Good," she said.

Once the street was empty, the next step was to start dismantling the houses. He began in December at the far edge of the cul-de-sac. It would be a controlled burn, he thought, and worried that someone would spot the smoke, then realized that even if they did, what were they going to do? There was no one to see it go.

He was sixty-three the year the river flooded — a century flood, worse than the previous year's century flood — and the municipality permanently ceded the village of Cowichan Bay to the water. Someone towed away the surviving float homes, but left the art galleries, the pottery studio, and the ice cream shop to the flood. At the end of the road to the estuary, he saw the eroded edge of cultivation, where the water had undercut the pavement, and the old cornfields were inundated with salt. He thought about fish and chips and cheap beer in the hotel when he was seventeen, back when they didn't card you and you could get Labatt's Blue for cheap while watching the sunset. The end of a day out on the water, a friend's dad's boat, a sunburn. Smoking cigarettes on a traffic barrier while girls in flip-flops walked down to rent a movie at the corner store, looking over their shoulders through their hair, laughing.

No one, he realized, not a single one of the kids he saw in town would ever have that, stupid as it was — those tiny moments of cigarettes and illegal booze and *Friday the Thirteenth* on VHS.

He walked home and dug another trench and planted a row of Oregon grape he'd been babying on his windowsill all winter.

In the winter of 2052, landslides blocked the highway north and south of the valley. The nights were so still he could hear fish jumping in the river if he held his breath, and when someone did start up an engine — maybe a chainsaw — the whine drew him outside in the misty hour. He strained his ears for that homely sound, conjuring in his heart the smell of diesel exhaust and sawdust.

He'd downloaded Wikipedia back when it was a manageable 20 TB, and at night — if he'd successfully charged his old battery — he'd trawl through that other world, reading about cities now drowning, and people long dead, and wondering about the kids he heard sometimes, saw sometimes in the distance but did not disturb, walking out from the reserve on Tzhouhalem road. He wondered at how small the world had grown for them, and how much wilder.

In the afternoons he tended the trees, talking to them like they might care about who lived here. He shared what history he knew: how the land had been a hillside, then a farm, then a subdivision where he and Jen had sat together under golden LEDs. He talked about Michelle and Chris, who always gave them smoked salmon at Christmas. Jim, with his immaculate and unnatural lawn. The Ervines with their elaborate jack o'lanterns.

The camas flourished and Bernard divided them, planting the fragile off-sets around the neighborhood. He tended the salal and salmonberry in what had been the Freemantle's backyard, where Octavia had gone for summer sleep-outs. At first, he pulled the blackberries, then he left them, on the principle that they were well adapted and delicious, and someone — someday — walking through the woods would see the trace of an old foundation and eat the fruit he'd left behind. He planted bitter cherry and crabapple. Soon after he stopped clearing the ditches or digging out the culvert, he watched the street become a seasonal creek at the bottom of his garden.

He was sixty-five when his last phone died, and with it the world again shrank, this time to the size of his memory, and the books that remained in his house. He still carried the phone with him, though, a comforting glass brick in his back pocket, which he'd instinctively grab to check for things he didn't know: how to make a smoker when his broke down, how to mend socks when they finally disintegrated, the species he saw and couldn't name, new ones arriving with changing temperatures.

When he'd collected enough questions — how do I do that? What is this? Where has everyone gone? — he walked into town to visit the library, and see if there was any government-issued flour. The kids he saw seemed rare and lonely, watching him, then disappearing among the unlit buildings if he walked toward them too quickly.

"Hey," he finally shouted when he saw a kid who didn't run. "Can I talk to you?"

The boy hesitated. He looked about ten, wiry and curious, with black hair cut in blunt bangs that hung into his eyes. At that age, Octavia had been all muscle, reckless, never walking when she could run or climb.

"My name is Bernard. I want to go to the library, but it's not in the same building I remember. Do you know where it is now?"

And now the boy relaxed, nodding. Together they walked along the railroad tracks toward downtown.

"I'm Benno," the kid eventually admitted, then went on to tell Bernard the kinds of things that are important when you're ten: about how he didn't go to school anymore, instead he went fishing with his dad but it was hard with the river full of junk up stream. How grandma grew the best blackberries ever and he was in charge of picking them . How he had a cat named Luna who'd just had kittens, three black and one tabby, and they hid in his shoes and purred if you even said their names, you didn't even need to pet them. It felt good to listen to this talk, the easy chatter of a child who was constantly amazed by what the world offered. He had missed this kind of conversation, leisurely and directionless, and he found he had things to tell Benno: about how the blackberries were good this year, and the fishing bad, how his childhood dog had been like that, too, wagging his tail as soon you said his name.

The library had been relocated to a bank downtown, the work of another old man who had transferred the digital catalogues to cards and guarded his shrinking collection with a terrible and stubborn silence. If people wanted to read, they brought him salmon, buckets of blackberries, batteries. People met there for news from an unreliable satellite uplink he maintained, rigged to a wind charger on the roof and solar panels in the parking lot.

"Benno," the old man said. "You here to read?"

"Grandpa, can I have a comic book?"

The kid settled down with an X-Men comic from twenty years before, while Bernard unleashed his questions: how to build a smoker, how to troubleshoot a solar cell array. Grunting, the librarian disappeared among the stacks. Bernard sat in the plastic chair near the window and read the bulletin board. They were all hand-written notices and offers of trade: fishing gear for camping stoves; an abundance of apples, a dearth of antibiotics; a boat leaving Cowichan Bay for the mainland, in search of paying passengers.

The librarian returned with an armload of books, including more comics.

As he searched, a new question occurred to Bernard. "What's the valley's population now?"

Benno's Grandpa shrugged. "Last official number was five thousand, but that's all estimates based on who knows what. Drones? Satellites?"

Bernard opened one of the books and saw the McPherson library stamp, and he was returned suddenly to his undergrad, sitting on the fountain outside McPherson, waiting for Jen. "UVic? How'd you get it?"

"I knew a dude. He sent us a ton of stuff when they dismantled the library. You'd be surprised who comes looking for books about gardening and first aid."

In the pile, he found a book full of drawings and photographs of living architecture: bridges made from the entwining roots of rubber figs, rooms grown from linden trees, branches trained onto forms to make benches. Furniture not built, but grown. There was an experimental barn, its walls made of branches tightly crossed in a diamond pattern, with a leafy roof. Fruit trees with ten different scions grafted to a single rootstock.

For a brief, flickering moment he imagined a world built not of plastic and concrete, but living trees: garden walls formed from intersecting branches, and a cathedral with a roof full of singing birds.

On the way home from town, he followed the old map in his head, but the road he took had been washed out in some flood, now scattered with bike tires and Christmas ribbons and lawn ornaments and bones. It was loud with the chuckles of chickadees, and the kronk-kronk of the raven overhead.

It was twilight and he was most of the way home when he noticed the flies, a cloud of them in the heat. Then he saw what they had settled on: the newly red and slick spine of some animal, the powerful bone of a thigh, in trampled earth stained darkly with blood. The color faded as evening crept on and he found himself suddenly still, but galvanized with a deep and wordless panic. He wanted to run but he knew he couldn't run, not yet.

He thought, I hope that kid is safe in his Grandpa's library, reading comics.

The next day, he found the golden arbutus on the south-facing slope just outside the subdivision. He'd never seen anything like it: it did not have the familiar red skin, but golden oval leaves and long trunks that twisted upward, more like muscled human limbs than branches.

His father had called arbutus junk trees that got in the way of the men who wanted cash crops like the Douglas fir. It was an unstable wood, harder than oak or maple. With a lathe and carbide blades, you could make a spoon, a Christmas orna-ment, but then the wood split and you had nothing. The living tree was different: if you carved a girl's name into a low-hanging branch — three easy letters, like J E N — you could return year after year to see it soften into the tree, growing smooth, like a scar on human skin.

He spent the next month planning, copying diagrams and text by hand before he returned the books to Benno's Grandpa. He found another golden arbutus up at the top edge of Michelle's lawn, where the forest thickened and you could look back down the hillside toward the water. That's where he'd start. It was a good place for a bench.

When the world ends, you lose track of important things: your wife's ashes, your daughter's location. It is important to be close to those you love, so you can reach out and touch them as the universe shrinks to a valley, a street, a room. A long time ago, the light hit the far reaches of the world, the dark side of the planet, which hummed even at night with people, with phones that would ring if one dialed their numbers. But since then the world has shrunk to what you can see if you climb the highest point of land and look into the next valley, or over the islands.

The light contracts, the distance recedes, and while you might trust the maps in your head, the coastlines have changed. The sea levels are rising, and the torrential winter downpours blow out roads and swell rivers. The deserts have expanded, and the lowlands are abandoned. Who knows what Venice looks like, or Jakarta? You can only see an eagle circling, diving for a Chinook fighting upstream in the Cowichan River, having dodged the hungry orca, the flotillas of sea lions who wait at the river's mouth.

Bernard had thought his private end-time would begin with an infected scratch. Maybe he'd fall and break his leg and then it'd be pneumonia. A cougar claiming the cul-de-sac for her territory. Dehydration in the arid summers, too tired to walk to the creek for water. Or beaver fever if he did make it there to drink.

It was none of these.

The smoke didn't surprise him, but his fear did. He had thought he had reached some state of exhausted resignation, but on seeing the leading edge of the fire climb the hillside toward him, his panic was animal. He had his bug-out bag at his feet, and a water bottle filled at the tepid cistern he'd rigged out back. The sky was dull, but the wind sharp and dry, feeding the fires as they burnt through what was left of the old world.

Where was Octavia right now, this second? He wondered why he had expected her to return after these crises ripped up the west, to get through the quarantine lines and the fires and the drought to find her way home, a tired figure with a backpack, in his mind always nineteen, as she had been when she left. But of course, where was home for her? She was on some northern homestead. Maybe she was in Toronto.

The wind rose, whirling sparks through the evening sky. Jim's house caught fire, and with it his store of firewood. He thought of running water, the tide rising across the salt-soaked fields of corn along the bay, the sea taking back the estuary. He thought of diving into the green quiet, where returning eelgrass and expanding oyster beds overtook the industrial trash of 150 years. A long time before, whole forests of fir and cedar had boomed there on their way to sawmills and lumberyards. He couldn't breathe. Summers down in Cowichan Bay, he'd take Octavia for ice cream and they'd walk the government wharf to see fishboats knocking gently against the huge, metal-flashed posts and smell the deep, salty breath of the undersea world. Now the sky was smoke-white, and so close he could not see the tops of the trees around the house. Now the sparks zoomed like fireflies through the darkening air and his fear was wild and hot and obliterating. He couldn't breathe. He thought of the waterfalls on the Malahat he saw from the back window of a car when he was a kid being driven south to Victoria. He couldn't breathe.

But there was Jen, coming in from the rain on a stormy night in November, the leaves dropping and the branches littering the roads, and her skin, when he kissed her, was cold to the touch, and streaked with raindrops. Her skin was cool and under his fingertips — her skin was — her skin — her —

In Tiangong, Noor passes over her hometown — Victoria, BC — every hour. If there's no cloud cover, she can find the familiar coastline and for a moment she can take in the whole range of her childhood and adolescence: her mother's house and the road on which she learned to drive, first dates, first lovers, excellent exam results, terrible disappointments. The park they hiked when she was twelve, where during camp-

outs she had seen the faint dot of the old ISS. All those experiences enclosed in such a tiny space, made even smaller when she looks over the edge of the Earth and sees the rest of the universe beyond.

Noor observes the milky grey streams that pour in a gyre across the north Pacific coast. It isn't the color that sets them apart, but their opacity among the otherwise luminous clouds. At night she can see through the thin spots to long lines of red moving inexorably across the rainforests.

That must be Portland, where her parents had lived before she was born. That is Seattle. She'd been at a conference at U of Washington, spoken to pre-med students about the international space program. That is Vancouver. She'd flown from YVR on her way to Hong Kong and then Kazakhstan. A man sitting beside her on the flight had said, it looks like Earthsea down there, all those green islands, and the white breakers. She'd nodded, yes, surprised by how right he was. Then the sun had set and the dark void of the Pacific had unrolled around the curve of the Earth, and she had tried to sleep sitting up in her cramped seat, but could not because Kazakhstan was waiting for her and then who knew what.

One morning in November — the third month of her rotation — clouds part to reveal the blackened coastline. She thinks of hungry deer in the valleys, and a cougar crouched in the dripline of burnt Douglas fir. She thinks of the sun over-head, a distant explosion that fuels them all, burning her shoulders the day she learned to swim at Sombrio Beach. She thinks of rain.

Above Tiangong is a web of satellites, run by the billion-aires who've collected in the climate havens of Detroit, Cincinnati, Toledo. Oceans climb the coasts, and methane belches from the permafrost, but techbros and their accomplices walk barefoot on native grasses that have been genetically modified to suit both drought and the inevitable summer downpours of the new Midwest. Beyond these refugia, much of the Earth below her is dark.

The following spring, Noor is back on Earth and working in the new headquarters in Cincinnati. In a photograph of the west coast, she recognizes the fine, defiant scrim of green growing over the blackened scars. Those are fireweed and blackberries. Those are alder saplings, and the re-emerging twigs of Garry Oak.

In the future this history will be captured through numbers so large they are unimaginable, measured from far away and high above the Earth: the hectares destroyed, the people who died and those displaced, the species lost, the rivers diverted. There will be maps recording the greatest extent of the burn, the way we now see maps of the Roman Empire under Trajan. It will — Noor hopes, though she is not naturally hopeful — be a shadow from which we'll emerge transformed. But looking over the salt deserts in the middle of Australia and the locust clouds over north Africa, she is afraid.

An Important Failure

It's 1607 (according to some calendars) and a falling cone from an elderly Pinaceae sitchensis catches on the rotting bark of a nurse log that sprouted while Al-Ma'mun founded the House of Wisdom in Baghdad. On this particular north Pacific island, the days are cold, and the water in Kaatza — the big lake near where this cone has fallen — freezes thick enough that one can walk out from the villages at the south-east end and look down to see cutthroat trout flickering underfoot. On the other side of the world, the Thames has also frozen, and stout winter children play across the canvasses of lowland painters, who preserve in oil the white-stained landscapes of northern Europe. In il Bosco Che Suona — the Valley of Song, the singing forest in the Alps north of Cremona where luthiers go to find their violins hidden in the trunks of trees — the winter is bitter, slowing the growth of Picea abies until its rings are infinitesimal, a dense tonewood unlike any material before or since.

Ninety years after the cone drops near Kaatza, Antonio Stradivari travels to il Bosco Che Suona on the old road from Cremona to select wood for his workshop. He rests his head against one trunk and listens to its cold history. This is the little ice age as written in the rings of a spruce tree. It sounds like a violin.

Jacob woke Mason after midnight. Ten minutes later, they walked out to the old truck, gassed up for the occasion, stale with multigenerational BO, since it had belonged to their grandfather before it was Jake's. The dusty fug was relieved by Sophie's botanicals: nasturtium; wood rose; one of her cash crops, a strain of CBD-rich indica she had been nurturing for years, called Nepenthe. They drove along the empty street, from the deeply green lakeshore to the old firebreak, gouged out of stone and clay twenty years before. Along disintegrating logging roads to the old burns where Mason could still see char. As kids, they had hiked here to secret rivers and camp-sites out of cell phone range.

Jacob drove in silence. Mason stared out the window at the ghost forest. Twice they got out to clear the road and Mason looked up into the low bush — blackened Douglas fir still towering over the blackberries and alder. Recovery plants, fast growing opportunists emerging from the last wildfire.

"Cougars?" he asked.

"A lot of them lately," Jacob said. "They've followed the deer. It's good news. But makes working at night a bit more exciting."

He thought he spotted its silhouette in the darkness above them and wondered what it saw, in turn — competitors or prey in the disorienting headlights. The eagles had come back, nest-ing in the ghost trees. So had black-tailed deer and robins. The microclimates had changed as the forests began their slow return, though, a prefigure of what the coast would be in a hundred years: arbutus further inland, outside its original ranges; Garry oak farther west and north as the coast dried out. In a thousand years, it would be another sort of forest. If it was still there.

In two hours they made it to the edge of the surviving rain forest, which — on the west coast of the island's mountains — had dodged the wildfires that destroyed most of everything else in the last twenty years. Twenty minutes on a rutted track, until they pulled over and met a guy, silent, nodding to Jacob as he climbed into the cab, directing them to an even narrower dirt track.

"This's Chris," Jacob said.

Mason-Chris nodded. So did the guy.

They weren't far from the tree, which stood in what was still a provincial park, technically, though the trails were rarely maintained, and what boot prints he could see were probably other poachers. This was the largest surviving Sitka spruce in the world, and maybe people still wanted to see it, even if the busloads of school kids were rare, and the marine biology station at Bamfield had been shuttered for years.

Three more men waiting. A few gestures indicated the direction they'd drop it. The time it would take. Mason-Chris hung back, watching the wiry old faller put on his helmet, his chainsaw beside him. They waited for the breeze to still. There was a kind of quiet he never felt in Vancouver, even now when it was marred by shuffling men. Or cougars. Then the chainsaw flooded them and he heard nothing but its whine as it cut through the trunk, kindred to the kind that grew in La Fiemme, the Valley of Song in the Italian Alps where — it was rumored — a skilled lumberman could hear a violin hiding in the trunk.

He'd heard there might be another ancient Sitka in Kitimat, but that was too far to travel, even for something as precious as old-growth tonewood. This one, though, he'd remembered visiting as a kid. Its size; the unlikely fact of its survival after two centuries of logging and wildfires.

It didn't take that long. A deep cut on either side in the direction of one of the other available roads, where a big truck probably waited. Then the wedges. The high, sweet note of the hammer. Waiting. Waiting. Until something inside it tore, and it fell, bounced, a thrash of branches like tendriled ocean creatures, or waves, like hair, like a body in spasm. Then it was still. Silence held for a moment longer, before they got to work limbing and bucking it.

Mason-Chris watched all the wiry, furtive men from — where? Port Alberni? Or maybe one of the transient camps, to which resource officers and RCMP turned temporary blind eyes because even they weren't assholes enough to burn down a five-year camp that had organized showers and a septic system built of old truck tires. As long as the outsiders kept their problems — opioids, smuggling — out of town.

"Deal with the stump," Jacob said.

Mason-Chris didn't know what that meant, so Jacob repeated, "Stump. Cover it over with whatever you can find on the ground."

"Is that really a problem? We're pretty deep in."

"They still send drones through."

"Why would they even — anyway, I need to —"

"— I'll get you when it's time."

Behind him, the stump was brightly pale in the darkness, sweet and resinous. He dropped branches over three meters of open wound, admiring the heartwood, which was surprisingly free of infestation, whether beetle or fungus. Behind him the tree grew steadily simpler, its branches tossed away, its trunk straight and handsome and more than four hundred years old. A baby compared to the ancient ones, the bristlecone or the big Norway spruce that had lived for nearly ten thousand years. But what would a bristlecone sound like? Sitka spruce, though, he had heard often and loved.

"— Chris."

He'd get to Cremona and apprentice to Aldo, because Eddie knew him and could write a letter. He'd visit the Valley of Song and see what survived of the European spruce, and he would tell the master luthiers this story of poaching old growth in a provincial park. They would laugh and clap him on the back and —

"— Chris. Come on."

Dragged away from his plans for Cremona and back to the immediate problem of sourcing old growth for a perfect violin, he saw that the tired, sweaty men had begun stripping their gear in the darkness, lit by phones and helmets. He didn't actually know what he was looking for, but he worked his way down the long, straight sections nearest the base, running his hands over the rough bark to look at the interiors by the light of his phone.

"This is it, Jake." he said without thinking. The group hushed. Ignored it. "This is the one."

The other guys melted into the darkness. It was close to daylight by then, and while the forest floor was still dark, Mason could see the sky for the first time since the clouds overtook the stars.

Jake squatted by the section.

"Are you sure?" he asked.

Mason tried to listen to it. Before the tree fell, he had felt alive to the world around him — the shudder of leaves, and the faintly padding feet of the cougar — but now the wood was inert. Whatever he thought he had heard — the thin high notes of a violin he had not yet built — had evaporated.

"Yes," he said. "I'm sure."

It took them two hours to get it to the truck. Then another three to get home.

"What'll happen to the rest of it?" Mason asked.

"Firewood went for thousand bucks a cord last winter. That tree could keep a lot of people warm. There's pulp, still. Mills will buy it up without asking too many questions. You don't get the same kind of cash, but it's safer and less work. And you know. Fentanyl. Or oxy."

Behind them, the quarter of old-growth spruce remained silent, except where the truck creaked in resistance to its enormous weight.

"There are luthiers around the world who would kill for that, in a few years."

"Sure. Or it'll heat someone's house this winter."

They made it home late that morning, their eyes gritty with exhaustion. Jake sat in the cab for a long moment, then said, "I'm going to grab a swim, then get to work in the greenhouse."

Mason knew he should help, but he found himself following the old route through the house to the bedroom he still thought of as his: the dark kitchen, past the bunches of garlic, the bookshelves in the living room piled with National Geographics from the twentieth century. Past the windowsills that still held grandma's things: Beach glass and thunder eggs. Feathers. Stained glass that caught no light in a window shrouded by bush.

He lay in the cool, stale room where the carpet had been discolored by water seeping through the wall forty years before. It smelled like being ten, like summer, like his mother. Like the thousands of nights his family had passed between the wood-paneled walls, the narrow window facing south toward Cowichan Lake — or Kaatza, as Sophie called it in keeping with her friends in the local band — out which they had all stared and wondered what would happen next.

During the Little Ice Age, global temperatures dropped about 1°C on average. There are debates regarding the causes of these aberrant winters. At least one trigger may have been the mass death of people in North and South America, where

ninety percent of the population, by some estimates, died after contact with Europeans.

Lost languages and cities; toddlers and great grand-mothers and handsome young men and dreamy girls; villages and trade routes and favorite jokes. After so many deaths, an area of agricultural land the size of France returned to forest. This re-greening sequestered enough carbon from the pre-industrial atmosphere that temperatures took centuries to recover and begin their steady rise to the present day. The wild and empty continent of later explorers was — in part — a sepulchre, a monument inscribed with languages they could not speak, a land populated by wit-nesses and widows.

From the cold and darkness of a hundred million deaths, to the chilly woodsmen of the Valley of Song, to Paganini playing il Cannone Guarnerius, it is a long and terrible history.

At Kaatza, the disaster is slow, despite temporary changes in climate, because the small pox that will ravage the coast has not yet arrived. People go about their business on the water and in the forest, from the Pacific coast to the Salish sea. Children are born. Songs are composed. The nurse log disintegrates. The little spruce rooted there rises toward the light, its heartwood formed in an apocalypse.

In addition to Nepenthe, Jake and Sophie grew a high-THC sativa, which Mason disliked because it made him paranoid, but which sold steadily as far away as Seattle, and kept — in Jake's words — the old homestead together. Sophie raised it hydroponically in Grandpa's old workshop, while Nepenthe grew in the market garden by the lake, catching southern exposure on a warm brick wall with the espaliered peaches and lemongrass.

Later that afternoon, Mason visited the piece under a tarp in a corner of the workshop. Mason had been greedy, and there was material for two-dozen violins, assuming he found within it the billets he needed. He tried to remember what Eddie had done the last time they toured the mills for legal maple, willow, and spruce. Eddie could hear a violin in a slab of big-leaf maple, could feel willow's sonic geometries as he tested its spring with his hands. If Eddie were here, the quarter would speak. He was still listening when Sophie shouldered through the door, a watering can in either hand.

"There are two more," she said, gesturing toward the door.

He grabbed them, warm with sunlight. Together they watered the market garden. Potatoes and tomatoes. Chili peppers and mint. And Nepenthe, the deep botanical fug of its leaves rising in the heat of the afternoon. Mason took cannabis oil away every visit, dropping onto his tongue in a resinous burn, applying the ointment to his right wrist where the tendons ached. More effective than anything he could afford legally.

"You ever going legit?"

Sophie shrugged. "If it hasn't happened by now, I doubt we'll ever get licensed. I applied again last year but never heard anything. Jacob said you got what you needed?"

Mason nodded, the tree crashed again through his mind.

"He's helping someone cut firewood. He said you should sleep while you can. How long do we sit on it, anyway?"

"It's got to season. A decade, probably. Ideally a century, but you know."

She nodded, then led him through the hydroponics to a tiny room full of geranium slips and tomatoes. "Lots to do, Mason. Keep watering."

Rebecca Campbell

In the third decade of the twenty-first century, a girl is born in Surrey Memorial Hospital. The labor is six hours. The child — magnificently named Masami Lucretia Delgado — has tiny, pointed fingers and strong hands that are precise in their movements, as though waiting for the fingerboard of a violin even in the moment of her birth. When she is three years old, an ad interrupts her cartoon, and she waits first in irritation, then in fascination, jabbing at the corner of the screen where the skip button should appear, but does not. Instead of a cartoon cloud who sings about rainbows and unicorns, she watches an ad for life insurance that features a little girl so like Masami, she seems to be a mirror, or a twin, with bright black hair and curious brown eyes. This little girl — the other Masami — holds a violin to her chin and plays something that makes Masami's heart rise in her chest. A white cloud drifting higher and higher among the rainbows.

Masami is too small to name what she hears, and though it marks her forever, she soon forgets this first encounter with destiny. Something of it must remain with her, however, because a year later she hears the sound of a violin and asks her mother, that, that, was is that?

She's four. Her father shows her violin videos. Outside the air is opaque with smoke from the fires in Lynn Valley, which systematically destroy the huge houses overlooking Burrard Inlet. The pipeline that terminated in Burnaby has cracked somewhere up-country, who knows where, and spilled two thousand barrels of diluted bitumen into a lake. But Masami is too small to understand, and when she hears the sound of Marguerite Fell playing the ex-Kajnaco violin — from a quartet made by Guadagnini in Milan in 1780 — she is transported, and some portion of her soul will never return from that transport. Her future is, at that moment, fixed. Her tiny hands will grow into her violin, the instrument less an exterior object than an extension of her body. She is, neurologically, emotionally, and psychologically, part violin. It's in her heart, in her muscle memory. By the time she's fourteen she'll have cubital tunnel syndrome and need regular physio to deal with nerve compression. Her body has grown up around the violin the way a tree grows over a nurse log.

Masami Delgado was the reason Mason poached the last of the ancient Sitka spruce. But it wasn't her fault.

Actually, maybe Eddie started it with one of those offhand comments about sourcing tonewood. Shuffling through the workshop in old jeans, pockets sagging with pencils and calipers, a finger plane. He stopped at Mason's bench, where Mason was mending a violin they got cheap from someone leaving town. He was still surprised to find Eddie trusted him to touch instruments. For a long time he'd just swept the shop floor, drove the van, tended the glue pot. He still did those things, but he also got to replace a split tuning peg on a student violin, and it felt good to hold it in his hands, feeling the thin shell of its body, saying to it, "Come on, little guy, let's get you sorted."

"It's never going to sound the same," Eddie said.

He listened to the long bow draw. "Yeah. It's not great. But it's solid for a student —"

"No," Eddie said, in the abrupt way that always left Mason feeling like he'd said something stupid. "No. It's the wood."

He ran his finger down the bright spruce face. "This is pretty young stuff. More carbon in the atmosphere changes the density of the wood. We're never going to see the same kind of old growth again, even if the forests recover. You need to drop the G."

Mason listened. Eddie was right.

That night Eddie took him along to hear Delgado play at the Chan Center, a rare treat, like the time early in his apprenticeship when he accompanied Eddie to hear Alu Vila playing

43

Bach on the ex-Norfolk, darkly redolent of 1805. Delgado had just received — for a three-year loan from the Canada Council for the Arts — the Plaisir violin of 1689, and had invited Eddie backstage to celebrate her first concert. Eddie, world-renowned luthier and representative of the CC, had been appointed its custodian for Delgado's term. She was thirteen. She played the Kreutzer Sonata.

"We're going to go check out the saddle," he said during the intermission.

"Why?"

Eddie shrugged, and the lights dimmed again.

Backstage, Delgado's parents hovered. Mason — still disoriented by the evening's performance — couldn't speak.

"May I?" Eddie said. She nodded. Her eyes never left the violin.

Mason screwed up his courage. "You have it for three years?" She nodded. "And then that's it?"

Her mother answered. "You don't get it twice."

It hurt him that something that fit so perfectly onto her shoulder should be lost. She should have it for the rest of her life, on international tours, and in recording studios. It should be hers by some right of genius.

"I wish," Mason said, "you could have it forever." But then Eddie was finished and her parents were shepherding her away, and he realized he hadn't heard her voice, not once.

As they waited for an Uber, Eddie said, "It's not going to last." Wildfires were burning on the north shore, and the sunset was an angry smudge. Mason thought about dying trees, and the sound of old growth leaving the world.

"What do we do?"

"Nothing we can do. The saddle's been wearing noticeably for decades now. Could be a split forming, though I didn't seen anything on the last CT scan. Maybe it'll show in the next twenty years. Or maybe it'll be longer than that. I don't know."

"We can't replace it?"

"We can. But we won't. They aren't immortal. Eventually it will be unplayable, and then it will go to sleep."

That night Mason walked down Granville Street past the shuttered theaters that had once been full of music. He circled back to Hastings, and walked out toward his little room in a building on Gore, where the rent was almost decent. Then he searched through Eddie's database and found the transcendental geometries of the Plaisir violin, emissary of the seventeenth century, where in the workshops of Cremona luthiers made instruments so perfect they seemed not to have been built, but grown. Alien seashells. The seedpods of strange flowers. He had touched one today, felt its lightness against his palm, patinated by centuries of sweat, the oil of many hands and faces, rich with life. All that alchemy of tree and climate, genius and history. She would have it for three years. Then the saddle would split, and it would be lost forever.

That was the day he formed the plan: a violin made as purely and patiently as he could manage, following the guidance of long-dead luthiers, passed down to him through Eddie. And when it was finished, he would got to the Po Valley and join the Scuola Internazionale di Liuteria Cremona, where he would tell a dozen old Italian masters the story of his accomplishment.

But the materials he'd need weren't just expensive, they were nonexistent. Trees of the five hundred ppm present wouldn't do. He needed old growth, with heartwood grown in the last climate minimum, when Kaatza froze and the last Viking settlement on Greenland disappeared under the ice. He needed Gaboon ebony, nearly extinct, smuggled out of Nigeria or Cameroon.

"Everything I can afford," he told Eddie the next day, "is ugly." Unspoken: too ugly for Delgado, who deserved more than the world could offer these days.

"Not ugly," Eddie said. "Different. But not ugly." He picked up the violin Mason had assembled from salvaged materials Eddie had discarded. Then he seemed to think, and he said, "Let me show you something," before disappearing up the stairs and into the shop, returning with a fiddle Mason had often looked at. A rough old thing, a curiosity.

"Some guy made this out of a post from a longhouse like a hundred and fifty years ago. If he can do that, you can figure something out."

The longhouse had stood in a long gone Musqueam village way down on southwest Marine Drive. The violin had a cedar front, a maple neck and back that Eddie insisted had come from a stack of firewood. He'd had some dendrochronologist look at it, dating the woods to the seventeen hundreds. Maybe some fiddler lost his on the crossing, or gambled it away, like in a song, but he'd landed on the edge of nowhere, and built something new from what he'd found. Not well built by many rules, and the sound was drowsy, sure, but deep, Mason could hear that just bowing the strings. He wondered what it would sound like in Delgado's hands. Something by de Sarasate. A Bach violin concerto. Or maybe it would be some dance number, once played in a small front room while the rain fell outside, and Vancouver wasn't even a city yet, a song interrupted, escaping from the violin when her fingers touched it. Maybe, he thought, it would be earlier sounds from an equally rainy night, a longhouse on the south slope toward the river, a rainy hillside that had not yet thought of becoming Vancouver. Voices. Laughter. A language he didn't know, and a moment captured in the reverberating matrices of the wood itself

A few weeks after he returned from poaching the giant spruce, and had begun to accumulate the necessary components for his violin, wildfires scoured the Fraser Valley and the north shore, and the smell of smoke brimmed his eyes with love and dread so he had to call them, just to make sure.

Still here." Jake said. "You okay?"

Mason could not answer that, because who was okay? No one was okay. Everyone was fine. "It smells like smoke here," he said. "Eddie's not doing too good with the COPD."

"Yeah?"

The world had smelled like this when he and Mom had arrived, grubby with two months in the emergency camp on Nanaimo's waterfront, waiting for the highways to reopen so they could go home. That's what Mom had said to him every night: we'll go home, soon. Not to the house in Cobble Hill, which was gone now, but out to the lake. To Grandma.

"Sophie wants to bring in trembling aspen for the other side of the firebreak, to slow the burn —" Here Jake went on at length about the plans to bring in a colony, borrowed from a stand downriver. Mason couldn't concentrate on what he said, but it was good to hear his voice and know that around him the house was darkening as the sun set, and outside you could, if you were lucky, hear the resident barn owl's nightly call. Sophie still at work in the garden, hauling wheelbarrows to the compost. In his smoky room, Mason's eyes ached until, finally, he wept.

Then, suddenly, Delgado was fifteen, an intensely silent teenager in heavy black eyeliner who wore combat boots in summer and rarely spoke when she came in for strings. Then she was sixteen and her time with the Plaisir nearly over, her parents joking tensely about how much it all cost — the travel, the extra tuition, the time.

Meanwhile, Mason made violins from the salvaged spruce and maple of a demolished bungalow on East Tenth, where he did some day labor for extra cash. In the evenings, he listened to each piece he'd nicked from the job, knocking it with a knuckle and wondering about its strengths, its provenance. He broke down a chest of drawers from Goodwill, scraping away the paint to show flamed maple. Oak flooring coated in decades of grime. A cricket bat made of willow, deeply scarred, might have provided the blocks he needed, but it was worm-eaten to the core.

He searched Stanley Park and found a shining willow near Beaver Lake, unusually straight. *Salix lucida lasiandra*, not the *Salix alba* preferred by the old Cremonese luthiers, but similarly easy to carve, and stable enough if he could find a straight length of trunk and season it properly. Resting his head against the trunk, he once again listened for the violin hiding within it, some sonic quality in the way it responded to his heartbeat, or his hand upon the bark.

He returned on a rainy night in January, alone, his back-pack damp and heavy with gear: A hacksaw. Rope. More than anyone in the world, he missed Jacob, who had always — even when they were both kids orphaned by fire and pandemic — been cleverer and stronger than he was.

He'd have to top it, which was a ludicrous endeavor, and he could hear Jake laughing, and their grandfather's anxious snort — the snort that meant, don't do it, kiddo. Despite the snort, Mason persisted. Willow was essential, and if he could snare vacant lot rabbits and skin them for glue, he could climb and top a willow, then walk back across town to Eddie's, where the wood might begin its secret transformation into something usable.

He'd climbed trees a lot as a kid. Higher even than Jake, who had a longer reach, but who was afraid of heights. It made them equals, according to Grandma. When he and Mom had arrived from the temporary camp in Nanaimo, after the rain hit in October and the fires down the coast died for the season, Jake was already there. He was waiting for his Dad to come back from the interior, where he'd gone to fight the big fire outside Princeton, when the dead pines went up like matches in the scorched afternoons. But he died by smoke inhalation on the side of a crowded road along with a hundred others, and Jake stayed, and later — when Mom left to look for work and caught the flu and died — the two of them lived like brothers.

Jake never talked about it, like Mason never talked about his mom, dying in the third wave of a new pandemic when he was seven, a few years after they'd landed back on the homestead. They all worked on the hydroponics in the workshop and the market garden on the south slope toward the lake. Weed was legal in the province back then, but the Cowichan Valley's economy was — by conservative estimates — still more than half dark, and mostly driven by small operations like Grandma's. And while he and Jake were orphans in a grow-op, Sophie was somewhere south of them in Langford, learning to garden with her grandfather. Eddie had just finished his years in Italy with Aldo, and was about to set up his own shop in Vancouver. Sophie studied horticulture on the mainland, then returned to Langford with a lot of knowledge and nowhere to turn it, until Jake found her on a beach in Sooke. Eddie won double gold at the Violin Society of America. Mason left school early for a cabinetry apprenticeship until a festival, where he picked up the unfinished body of a fiddle — spruce, maple, willow — and found the thing he was made to do.

All those people — those accidents — led him here, after midnight in the shivering wet of a rain forest park in November, and he was older than he liked to admit. Nevertheless, he pulled himself up to the lowest branch, then struggled from handhold to foothold until he was high enough to cut, relieved when the unusually straight center fell with a sound that was both troubling and familiar, the tree swaying in response to the dropped weight. He descended, limbed it, bucked it in convenient lengths, and packed five of them in his truck. Then, looking up, he saw a straight branch just below his cut, and he could not resist it. He remembered Jake's wrinkled look of dread when they climbed too high, his warnings. "Do you know what could happen?"

"I know," Mason said, and swung up into the willow. He was a couple of meters up when the branch on which he stood — one hand snaking around to grab his hacksaw — snapped. Willow is a brittle, fast-growing tree, splendid in its youth, but

49

soon senescent. This one, more than fifty years old, could not support a man's weight a second time that night.

The ground was wet and spinning and he said, as though someone might be there, "Help me, help me," and he thought of his mother, standing just behind his shoulder, about to answer him, pick him up, carry him home. But she wasn't, of course, so he lay still until the ground righted itself, and the pain steadied: not faded, but no longer in crescendo. He could still move his toes. Then he found he could stand. His left shoulder screamed, but his left fingers could move. He hauled himself fifty meters to Pipeline Road and called an Uber. It was nearly a week's wages to get back home.

His shoulder never healed properly: a new MRSA at the hospital, one without a name that hung out in the linens. Not one of the virulent kinds that kills you in two days, but the other ones, that persist under the skin. There was an open sinus that ran from the outer edge of his shoulder, right above where the bone had cracked. It was three months before he could work again, but Eddie kept his place, and emergency dis-ability got him through, though he didn't eat much once his savings ran out.

When he told Jake the story — a joke, look what I did, what would Grandpa say — Sophie threatened to come over and look after him, and when he refused she sent him Nepenthe. A few weeks out of the hospital and he could move his left arm enough to dress himself, and Eddie helped him put Sophie's ointment on his left shoulder. He smoked it, too, in the basement in front of his workbench, the deep, slow breaths easing his shoulders out of their hunch, until he felt almost okay. By then Delgado's term with the Plaisir had ended, and she celebrated those three glorious years with a last concert at the Chan Center, for which Mason had a ticket, and which he missed because he was still in the hospital.

"Don't worry," Eddie told him. "There's a recording."

"You know what I mean."

"I think it's going to Prefontaine. A kid in Saskatoon. He's good."

"But what's she going to play?"

Eddie shrugged. "There are a lot of beautiful violins."

"No." Mason said, in rare disagreement. "There aren't."

He ran into Delgado's father on the street, once. "She won't touch a violin. It's been six months."

"She's probably —"

"— all she does is play video games. She's staying out. She's so angry."

He said more about her laziness and rage, then he had to be somewhere and Mason just stood there, blocking traffic on the sidewalk, thinking of Delgado speaking bitterly and at length about the globe's many failed revolutions, her rapidly narrowing future, and he wanted to tell her: please wait, just a little longer, for me to finish it.

A year later she received the extraordinarily fine ex-Jiang violin from an anonymous donor. He went to hear her play Bach at the Orpheum Theater, with the Vancouver Philharmonic accompanying. She was eighteen. When she came into the shop, she smiled through the eyeliner, and he asked her, "Where next? Buenos Aires?"

"I haven't seen you in weeks. What happened to your shoulder?"

"I fell weird. Not Buenos Aires? Singapore?"

"Oh. Yeah, it's hard to rationalize unless you've got a lot of work. I might be playing a gig in Toronto next year. And I was down in Seattle."

"Recording, then?"

"Maybe. I'm working on early childhood education."

"Oh," he said, surprised. "Oh. Cool."

"Eventually it'll be music therapy. Gives me something to do with the lessons Mom and Dad paid for."

It hurt him to hear that, though he didn't know if that was some pain she felt but did not speak, or whether it was his own hope, which he did not like to acknowledge, for fear of smashing it. That she'd get another term with the Plaisir. That when she was finished with it, he'd present her with his own creation, and her career would be transformed as the violin opened up, becoming something new as she played it. He had not imagined her in a classroom with toddlers, playing "Pop Goes the Weasel" while they marched in circles around a bright orange carpet. But neither had he imagined himself working for Eddie for his entire adult life, and here he was.

For a few years after the fall, he made nothing new, just ran the shop and stirred the glue pot, and made sure that Eddie took his meds and saw his doctor. But as his arm recovered, sort of, and he no longer dreamed of falling, he could stand to look at the willow again. He could even look at the old Jack Daniels box in a corner of the storage room, which held the violin in its constituent parts. You could mistake it for kindling, if you didn't know.

It still took him three years to open the box and begin work on the forms, slowly because his left shoulder remained weak and sometimes his left hand failed. But for an hour sometimes, in the evenings, he worked ribs and blocks of willow in the basement workshop at night, where he often stayed on a cot in case Eddie needed help.

It took another five years of austerity to pay black market prices for Gaboon ebony from Nigeria, the whole time worrying the trees would all be dead before he could save the money. In the end, the wood he needed for the fingerboard, tailpiece, and saddle cleaned out what was left of his Cremona account. But he saved money on the tuning pegs, which were boxwood poached from Queen Elizabeth Park and stained a fine black.

By then, Mason had moved into the shop — temporarily they said — to keep an eye on Eddie, because he'd got old. He'd always been old, in Mason's mind — fifty when Mason joined the firm at twenty-two, but not old old. Now he shuffled around the workshop, skinnier every year, quieter. Pretty soon he stopped going down to the basement because of the stairs, so Mason set his workbench up in what had been a dining room. Eddie could still watch the till, but he hardly spoke to customers, and he was happiest at the bench in his dressing gown, working on some delicate job, listening to the grubby speakers that sat on the kitchen counter.

Once while they were having coffee, Eddie reached across the table for a spoon and his wrist emerged from the ragged cuff of his hoodie. Mason was transfixed by how thin it was, how the skin had begun to pucker and spot, the careful way he picked up the spoon, as though every action required some calculation.

"What are you now, seventy?" he said without thinking.

"Dude. I'm seventy-six."

"Oh," Mason said. Thought. "Then I must be — shit."

Eddie laughed. Coughed. "Yeah. Exactly."

That sweltering July, he salvaged broad-leaf maple from an antique dresser and began shaping it into the violin's neck. A king tide rolled over the flats by the hospital and the science center, creeping over the grass below the planetarium and flooding Jericho Beach, where a long time ago Mason had milled with the festival crowds listening to music. After he left the skytrain station, he walked toward False Creek and watched a river otter slip across the concrete walkway and into the water, untroubled by the disaster, just like the seagulls or the ducks. But then he saw a dogfish, dead on the concrete, like it had thrown itself over the railing. When he looked up, he realized there were more, some of them twitching, arching

53

their backs as though they could throw themselves into the water again. He thought of worms on the sidewalk after rain, and just as he had when he was little, he picked it up, avoiding its dorsal spines. Its tiny shark-eyes were so full of rage it would stab him through the hand if it could, but instead it wriggled its tense, muscly body until he threw it back over the railings, where it twisted in the air, then disappeared under the murky water.

West of Vancouver island's Pacific coast, a blob of warm water forms and grows from summer to summer. The mola mola follow its high temperatures north to Alaska. Fleets of Velella ride the winds to shore, and turn the beaches of Tofino and Uclulet blue-grey, where the remaining tourists walk barefoot along the sand, wondering if this is, finally, the apocalypse they've been waiting for. It is not.

At Sombrio Beach, a little girl named Erin walks barefoot in the sunrise, picking her way from the dry forest where her family has pitched their tents to avoid the king tide that has worn away the shore. She steps onto the firm, cool sand and looks northwest, where she can see open ocean through the mouth of the Strait of Juan de Fuca, where the Salish Sea crashes into the Pacific, and she thinks of what her mother told her, about how squinting in that direction took your eyes all the way to Japan around the curve of the Earth. How fishing boats and glass floats and nets wash up on the western coast of the island, and they have traveled a thousand kilometers, a distance she has seen on a map, but cannot imagine. There are some pokey rocks here. They hurt. Her ankle is red where she slipped against a barnacle the day before and gashed the skin. She bends to scratch it, and when she stands she looks north along the beach, toward the

Pacific, and sees the first dolphin as a wave unrolls and the white foam drains away from this clumsy grey body, pushed ashore by the prevailing winds. She does not recognize it at first, though she has seen their fins before on rare days, three or four in a pod, rising and diving and seeming to play in a way she appreciates as a seven-year-old. She sees another lump. And another. She stops her careful progress toward the water, and stares at the animals, unable to comprehend what she sees. There is a chaos of fins off shore, rising and diving and falling toward the land.

He went back to the shop to tell Eddie about the first finger of floodwaters sliding across Main Street and about the fish. The fifty centimeter that had been long predicted, then another half-meter from a king tide, and here we were, in the future, watching mussels grow over the bases of pillars that previously upheld shades over the park benches of wealthy Yaletown residents. He wanted to say to the walls that had once con-tained False Creek: turn it back.

He got home to find Eddie listening to Melchior play the Bach exercises on the Bourbon viola. Mason stowed the billets in the basement workshop. He could hear Melchior upstairs while he did it, louder than Eddie usually did, so some of the low notes rattled the door to the workshop.

Up the stairs, eyes still full of the floodwaters engulfing Main Street, he stopped in the doorway about to spill his news and said, "What's wrong?"

Wildfires in the Po Valley, burning farms and groves left dry by a five-year drought. Cremona engulfed, and at least a thousand people dead. The Museo del Violino lost, and a pietà, a portrait of St. Sebastian from a small town. An altar piece and a collection of fine instruments stored in Torino.

"No more Cremona," Eddie said. "I should have asked Aldo last week —"

Melchior filled the tired silence.

"I wish," Eddie said in the torn voice of a night spent coughing in the lumpy old futon chair in the corner of his room, which bore the dark marks of his hands where he had been resting them for forty years. "I wish I'd enjoyed it all more."

"I don't —"

"— I mean, sure I should have done more to change things and been a proper revolutionary or whatever the fuck. But actually I just wish I'd spent less time thinking about it, and more — I miss coffee, you know? Really good coffee and drinking it in a coffee shop. I miss knowing I could get on an airplane at any time and go to Cremona and see Aldo, just to see him. I don't think I enjoyed it enough. And here we are. And it's too late."

"It's not too late," Mason said.

"No more elephants. No more ebony trees."

"It's not." He thought of the silence after the chainsaw, and the men who waited as the spruce fell, cougars moving soundlessly in the tinderbox woods around them. He thought of the storm of its branches hitting the ground, and the way it shuddered under his feet, and how he had found it, the core pieces, the heartwood of his violin, which had been alive in the seventeenth century, and which had waited on a hillside until now.

First Eddie laughed, "Oh, dude," he said, and coughed.

Mason thumped the old man's back with his good arm, still saying, "It's not too late."

He couldn't explain it because they had arranged a silence regarding the violin, and the things he did to build it. He couldn't explain, but it wasn't too late because under a tarp in a shed, in that bit of land between the lake and the ghost forest, the spruce had been seasoning for fifteen years. In a box under his workbench he had black market Gaboon ebony for

56

the fingerboard, one of the last shipments smuggled out of Nigeria: fine-pored, dense, deeply black ebony. He had glue made from the skins of rabbits he had trapped at night. He had carved the geometrically perfect scroll of its neck from a piece of two hundred year old big-leaf maple. And soon, soon, he would bring them together into something miraculous.

It must happen soon though, Mason knew, looking down at the old man, his lips and chin slick with sputum coughed up in the last paroxysm.

"You look like your dad," was the first thing Jacob said to him when, late on the third day of travel, he reached the house by the lake, slack-jawed and greasy-haired (once that trip had been measured in hours, you could be there and back in a day). It had been fifteen years since his last visit. His shoulder — numb with the weight of his backpack — twitched in its socket, swollen and tender. He was limping, too, by the time he made it to their gate.

"I feel like I got old like, suddenly. How's Sophie?"

"Great," she answered. Mason started. In his exhaustion he had not realized that the frizzle-haired figure in the doorway was Sophie, the greenish light of the lantern casting her face in craggy shadows and lines. "Yeah, we age hard now," she said. "But that's everyone. And your shoulder's still bad. I'll look at it."

They lifted his backpack, then helped him with his shirt. Sophie's sweet, botanical scent and her fingers overtook him, then a hot cloth washing away the dried fluids that had seeped from the open wound in his shoulder.

"It's an abscess," she said. "But I imagine you know that. Do you still have a doctor? Are they giving you anything? I don't like the smell."

He no longer had a doctor, but the guy at the clinic helped sometimes. "Nothing to do except surgery."

Then the heavy skunk of Nepenthe overtook the ache, a scent that reminded him of his grandmother's garden on a hot day, penetrating and astringent beneath the peppermint and lemon balm.

"It smells like —" he said in a voice that seemed to come from far away, but he couldn't tell them, exactly, what it smelled like. Like home, maybe. Like his mother, when he had a mother. Then they helped him to the old back bedroom. He didn't remember anything after that.

When he woke shortly before noon, Sophie was gone but Jake was there on the porch outside the kitchen, drinking something sort of like coffee made out of toasted barley.

"She's been working with the Forestry Lab at UVic on some trees," he explained. "Someone she knew in undergrad got ahold of her and they've been working together. Genetic mods. Fast growing. Carbon sinks. Drought resistant. It's promising."

It was the first good news Mason had heard in a long time. Together they walked up to the gardens she'd been building on old house sites. The street still showed traces of tarmac, if he kept his eyes fixed on the remaining yellow street paint. If he looked between his feet and listened to Jacob talk, and felt the lake breeze, the town could be as it was when he was a kid. Maybe. Or when his mother lived here before the fires. Or before that, when their grandparents built this homestead at the edge of nowhere and Ts'uubaa-asatx kids played in the lake.

But then, Ts'uubaa-asatx kids still played in the lake, and white kids, and the Sikh kids had returned to Paldi when the village grew up around the temple again. Kids climbed through the alders that grew in the path of old fires, picking black-berries rich with the heat of a new world. Kids fishing and weeding garden plots where the houses had been demolished. Kids singing songs he didn't recognize.

Jacob was limping slightly now. They stopped when they saw Sophie in the middle of a garden near the water, her hair a frizz of gray in the sunlight, and a couple of boys and girls nearby, their arms full of green. Her hands were dirty, right up to the elbows, and when she saw them walking toward her, she waved the carrot tops she held.

"Rajinder brought some Jersey cows from up-island," she explained. "They like the carrot tops. It's our turn to get a couple of liters. The butter is ah-fucking-mayzing."

Together they walked home along the lake, admiring the late afternoon sunlight. "The arbutus look good." Mason said.

"They have lots of space since the fires. There are a few of these around, too." Here Jake grabbed a branch of a young tree, pulling it back to reveal the trunk's gold skin.

It was beautiful. Mason crouched to touch it, pearly and smooth, not like bark at all. "What are they?"

"A mutation? Some GMO from one of the forestry programs? It grows fast, like all the carbon sequestration species."

Arbutus was a stubborn, reactive tree, its trunk often twisted to escape the shade of Douglas fir. That tension remained long after the tree had been cut, seasoned, and found its way to a carpenter. The original twist returned in the form of checks and splits and warps, like a memory. Either you waited five years or you worked it green and took whatever the wood gave you. Once he turned a bowl from newly-cut arbutus and watched it warp from a perfect circle, the edge checked and separated along the growth rings. He'd tossed it, but now he considered that his work had revealed the tree's disobedient history: its dry seasons and its floods, its branches in search of sunlight, the salt that poisoned its lower limbs.

"Good for the stove, though," Jake said, echoing their grandfather who always had it on the woodpile.

The sapling before him wasn't *Arbutus menziesis* as he had known it when he turned the bowl that broke itself under the pressure of its own history. The growth pattern was similar: a cluster of trunks from a shared root, that would grow into a tree with naked lower limbs and an airy canopy.

He kicked at the soil over its roots.

"I think it propagates by runners," Sophie said. "It's clonal as far as I can tell, like aspen, and it roots easily from cuttings. I've never seen anything like it."

That evening they ate a soft farmer's cheese from Rajinder's herd, and she talked about the trees, the plantation on the old townsite, about more plans with Ts'uubaa-asatx Nation, a gang of kids who were salvaging what they could, then replanting the burned-out subdivisions from twenty years before. You couldn't see the old roads in some places, she said. It's like they're gone.

"Where?"

"Everywhere," she said. "It's the regreening. We lost what, ninety percent of our population to the mainland? So why not give it all back? Some of the Cowichan kids started it in the subdivisions nearer the coast, torching the houses last winter. Give it a couple of hundred years, and people will be making violins from the trees we're planting."

He didn't want to say it, but her newly wild world — without roads, without houses — filled him with a terrible bitterness he could not describe. "They won't sound the same," he said.

"Nope," Jacob said. "Not at all the same."

That night he lay a long time in the half-sleep of pain and painkillers, his shoulder numb from Sophie's ministrations that evening. He could not escape the crash of the old Sitka spruce hitting the ground, the crunch of five hundred years of upward growth giving in, finally, to gravity. He wondered if it would still be standing if he hadn't mentioned it to Jake fifteen years ago, in the middle of the night, when he was going to demolition sites looking for old spruce and wild with ambition for Delgado, who would play Moscow and Barcelona and Singapore. Jake had asked where it was: Did he remember how to get there? Could he find it on a map?

Mason did remember, and said I'd like to be there. I'd like to listen to it. A couple of months later, Jake had mentioned it again, and here we are, he thought, his shoulder throbbing dully on the other side of Nepenthe.

The day Mason returned from the island, Eddie woke him up just before midnight, when it was still hot and airless.

"I gotta. Go. In —" he said.

"Where?" Mason asked, stupidly, then realized what Eddie meant, found his shoes and helped the old man down to the curb, where they waited for an Uber, then waited at the hospital for seven hours, Eddie silent, breathing roughly in, and raggedly out again, while other patients paced, sometimes shouted, and a fluorescent tube above their heads flickered and hissed.

They kept him in for a couple of days. When Mason visited him with things from home — his tablet, a sweater, a newly refurbished violin for inspection — he was a shrunken, cranky man, complaining to the nurse in a small, petulant voice. It was so hot. Could they do something about it? The heat.

Mason sat with him while he ate, then walked an hour back to the shop, where he had set up a bed in the basement, the nearly-cool room that smelled of wood shavings and resin and glue, which was comforting while — on the other side of the peninsula — Eddie struggled with each breath in turn. Here it was almost quiet. Just Mason and the remaining problem: the sound post. Properly speaking, it should be made of spruce, like the front, but he wanted something that had seasoned longer than fifteen years. Something precious to hide away, something only he would know about.

There was the old fiddle, the one some frontiersman made out of wood salvaged from the skids that once ran through

Gastown and the beams of longhouse. Once, shortly after he met her, Delgado came into the shop for an order of strings and Eddie brought it out. She played "Where Does That River Run?" and he had laughed, and asked her to play again, anything, to wake the violin up and keep it alive a little longer. She had played at length and with wild generosity: sweet old waltzes; the Québecois "Reel de Napoleon;" a Cape Breton lament.

Humming, he climbed the stairs. He let himself into the shop and opened the display case that held the old fiddle.

It was another crime. Nevertheless, he carried it downstairs to his bench. He did not want to think too much, so he worked quickly: pulling the old sound post out and adding a new one, returning the violin to the store's display case. Downstairs, the old bit of dowel was rough against his fingers. Cedar, maybe from the same post in the longhouse on the Fraser, light and ancient and marked by the original luthier's rough knife. Fragrant when he warmed it with his hands, but no potent aromatics, just a deep and redolent dust.

Then he fitted it, and it hid so perfectly in his violin, maybe no one would know the terrible thing he had done, the secret history he had stolen like all the other secret histories that constituted his violin. He knew, though, all the courses that materials took, from Nigeria, from the islands, from demolished bungalows in east Van, from vacant lot rabbits, and from Stanley Park.

Even from his bed, even on oxygen, Eddie was critical when Mason brought it upstairs, examining it with an eyeglass until he conceded that the sound was as fine, in its own way, as any number of other violins he'd seen. Finer, even, than the composites he'd started to use for his own work (when he could work), corene and carbon fiber.

"You made something, kid." It had been a long time since anyone had called him kid, even Eddie. "Does it have a name?" Eddie asked.

"Does it need one?" If it had to be named it should be something elegant and sonorous. Kiidk'yaas. "I don't know. The Vancouver violin."

"Better than that."

Eddie wouldn't play it, and neither would Mason. Delgado was swamped at the center, and had a toddler, so while the violin — Spruce Goose? — was finished in September, they didn't hear it until the New Year.

She was late. That was okay. The toddler was with her, which was slightly disturbing, but Mason figured they could keep her away from the detritus of the apartment, which was mostly workshop. And there were dry little cookies, at least, to feed her, at the back of a kitchen cupboard.

"I meant to leave her at home, but you know Johnny got a last minute shift —"

"No worries," Eddie said, quietly because he could only speak quietly now. "We're just happy to see you."

"This is it?"

Mason's throat was unaccountably closed, so he just — Delgado juggled Belinda from one arm to the other. "Oh," she said. "Oh."

"Mommy?" Belinda murmured, sleepy.

"I'm going to put you down for a sec."

She rubbed her hands on her jeans, Belinda now squatting at her feet, leaning on her knee.

"Oh," she said. He thought he saw a tremor. Her face dropped into her neck, so her hair fell forward and she looked as she had when she was fourteen and coming into the shop for new strings special-ordered from Berlin, talking about Bach.

Then the bow drawn across the open E, and he heard it, the sweetly deep, the brightly clear reverberation. Delgado made a wild little laugh and ran a scale, another scale, then interlocking arpeggios. Ševčík.

At her feet, Belinda spoke to a little blue bear, patting her threadbare ears.

Delgado dropped the violin from her neck, cradled it. Her eyes were bright, as though with tears, but her voice was warm.

"It is — oh, Mason!"

"Will you play something?"

She played Beethoven. The Kreutzer Sonata, as though she remembered the night that had stuck forever in Mason's heart: the Chan Center, and the Plaisir violin, and Delgado. Eddie leaned to the left side of his wheelchair, his eyes closed, the oxygen tank hissing faintly, the sound of people at the window, Belinda's murmurs to Bear. All these interruptions should be maddening, but they were not, and only seemed to complement the room's fragile magic.

When she was finished, she sat heavily on the remaining chair.

"How long have you been working on it?"

"A while," Mason said and saw her as she had been, fifteen and brilliant with an actual future stretching all the way to Paris. He had imagined hearing it for the first time in some acoustically perfect opera house, because the world would have recovered by then. He knew it was foolish, but it hurt to think Delgado would never carry it away from this provincial little corner.

"What will you do with it now," she asked, a wobble in her voice, the harmonics of longing. "Who'll play it?"

It was strange to him that she needed to ask.

"No," she said when she understood. "Oh no. No."

Belinda looked up from Bear. "Mommy. Mommy?"

"You can use it in your classroom, can't you? I think it'll age okay. It'll open up."

She didn't respond for a minute, but crouched down to where Belinda sat with Bear, her brow furrowed with worry for her mother. Then she stood and asked, "Does it have a name?"

"See? It should have a name," Eddie said.

Mason heard the oceanic crash of falling spruce, his own cry as he hit the dirt at the base of a shining willow in Stanley Park. The market garden and the homestead, the lake, the abandoned subdivisions and the burn lines that still showed through the underbrush, the ghost forests, the dead black teeth of what had once — a long time ago — been a rainforest. And among them, Jacob still cutting lumber and helping out at the garage when he could, fishing and hunting. Sophie in the greenhouses and the gardens, with her new Garry oak trees and her transfigured arbutus, the beetle-resistant spruce that would never, ever, be the kind of tonewood he wanted. The firebreaks of trembling aspen, the return of cougars. The steady erosion of human shapes: foundations and roads all lost to the burgeoning forest.

"Nepenthe?"

As he said it, he wasn't sure what it meant: a physick that would make the end easier; a draft of healing medicine.

"Nepenthe." Eddie said. "There it is."

"Remember," Sophie had said before he left. "You're going to come back here for good, eventually. It's still home."

Unspoken: come back when Eddie has died and you're ready to give up on global dreams and figure out how to live out the rest of your days in this shopworn future.

He had just nodded through the ache of disappointment that had accompanied him for decades now. But a tiny, exhausted part of him almost liked imagining it, how he'd go back to work in the garden, raising saplings for the new forest that even now overtook the old world, watching kids disappear into the wild.

Masami Lucretia Delgado plays the Nepenthe violin daily for forty-five years, even if it's only ten minutes when she gets home from work, her kids playing noisily outside the bedroom. Five minutes before everyone else is awake, Belinda fourteen and saying Mom are you seriously playing right now? She plays it on the day they leave their apartment because the seawall at the mouth of False Creek has failed. She plays it in the back of a car as they drive inland, toward interim housing in which they'll live for five years. Nepenthe is a fixture in the temporary-but-actually-permanent school she establishes in a slipshod village on the Fraser River. Together, she and Nepenthe accompany Belinda's wedding, and Masami's grandchildren fall asleep to lullabies from those strings. Despite her daily practice, she will never hear its most perfect expression: the violin will be its best long after the maker is dead, and the first hands that played it are too crippled by arthritis to make more than sighs. But she will play on while she can, because the violin must not go to sleep, and the longer she plays it, the more the alchemy of sound — the resin, perhaps, the glue, the cellular acoustics of the wood itself — will transform the object, preparing it for its ultimate player. Maybe Belinda will first hear the violin open up into its richest, fullest tone. Maybe it will be her son. Or maybe someone a hundred years in the future, who lives in a different world than we do, but who will pick up the instrument and draw her bow across the strings, releasing the reverberations of a thousand thousand crimes and accidents into the singing air.

Scions and Root Stocks

Kit George was born in October 2055, the same week a wildfire leveled 150,000 hectares between Parksville and Port Alberni. The fire ended with one of those sudden autumn storms, but by then it had razed Cathedral Grove, a rare, old growth refugio where Douglas fir had stood for nearly a thousand years, which had been carefully defended against earlier fires. That storm was only the beginning. An atmospheric river flooded the coast from Puget Sound to Port Hardy. Without roots to fix them against the weight of water, the treeless hillsides slid into the old logging roads and creek beds, collecting in debris flows that destroyed half the bridges on the island highway.

The week of Kit's birth, the storm that stopped the fires north of the Cowichan Valley also loosened the hillsides denuded by an earlier fire, and heavy clay flowed into town. The Cowichan River cut new channels through what had once been the mall parking lot and the highway through town. Kit was born in the front room of his grandparents' house, attended by his aunts and his grandmother, while outside smoky rain pummeled the streets. Leaving the room to breathe before the final push, Kit's father smoked and wondered what he could possibly find to give his kid in the ashy, changing world.

When he was a little boy, Kit asked about the day he was born, and what town had been like before that: the traffic lights, the mall with Santa at Christmas. He was hungry for stories, and when he was tired in the dark winter nights, he rested his head on his grandmother's shoulder and said, "tell about the olden days." When he was old enough to notice the world around him, he saw blackened and treeless hills ringing the valley. When he could walk, he saw them green with broom and blackberries, fireweed and goldenrod. Kit grew up among the successional species: fast-growing alder, big leaf maple. When he was six, he walked beneath young cottonwoods that grew along the riverbank studded with the remains of the old world: shreds of plastic still brilliant, metal cars rusting. By the time he was ten, those remains were overgrown with ivy and nettles, but he nevertheless remembered them, and the world that existed only in stories.

Kit worshiped Benno because he could make photovoltaic cells out of salt and copper, though he preferred to mend what they already had rather than — as he put it — make something a quarter as good and ten times as difficult. He'd grown up in his grandpa's library, reading everything he could find that had the UVic stamp in the flyleaf. When he was seventeen, he'd crossed the Salish, island hopping to Friday harbor, then Anacortes, and traveled south to Seattle to see what they'd done with the old tech headquarters, abandoned when the big corporations relocated to Cincinnati and Detroit. He'd stayed in Seattle a year, learned about recycling electronics, talked with the farmers who took over city parks and the university's experimental farm on Lake Washington, who had planted the rich bottomland of south Seattle. He came back home to Cowichan land full of ideas. He was the one who'd started the demolition projects in the abandoned suburbs. All by himself at first.

Benno could smoke salmon and rewire an old satellite uplink to get news from Korea and Australia. He could play "It's All Still Fine" on his guitar and he sounded — Kit was pretty sure — like a rock star. Once during a demolition, he had carried a pane of glass out by himself, and it had shattered across his back. He still bore the fine, white scars on his shoulder and throat, though someone had gone through each cut with tweezers to pull the glass, and Benno survived it all, with nothing but a few swigs of booze to keep him calm. He liked to tell dirty jokes when the surveyors were tramping out into the wet suburbs of the valley, before the demolition crew. To keep their spirits up, he said, though Kit died of embarrassment when Benno laughed and snorted out a punchline that inevitably involved boobs.

But Benno remembered the old world: electricity and gasoline and soldiers coming in to clear roads or fill sandbags along the river. He remembered Canada. Just like his grandpa, he collected books, and read about bailey bridges and wind chargers and batteries and satellite networks in the sky overhead.

When Kit was sixteen, Benno tapped him for the survey group and made him memorize an extensive list of necessary salvage: copper wire and unbroken windows; concrete block foundations and brick walls. The first summer, Kit always missed something, which was why he had to stick with Benno, walking the streets of dead suburbs together, each list he made corrected in irritating detail.

At the front door of a huge house, cavernous, its pressboard walls showing grey through gaps in the shingles, Benno asked: "Okay kid, what do you see?"

Kit was honest: "A fucking disaster."

"No. What do you *see*?"

"Like. A *house.*"

"What is it made out of?"

"Dude, I don't —"

"— bricks? Glass? Concrete? Gypsum? Aluminum? What about copper? Are we going to get any wiring out of it?"

Kit sighed in the way grandma hated. "Just tell me what you want to get."

"The flooring is all vinyl. We can take that."

"Can't we just burn it down?"

Here Benno sat abruptly on the concrete step. Kit joined him, sitting at his feet like a little kid.

"Kit. If we want to survive this, we have to be wild and smart and we have to use every fucking thing left to us. And part of that is plate glass from a house some bougie asshole built fifty years ago."

The cold soaked from the concrete through the seat of Kit's old jeans. Jeans worn by a hundred other butts before they even got to his.

When Benno spoke again his voice was gentler: "We've lived here for ten thousand years. Someone survived everything history threw at them, the fires and tsunamis, the earthquakes, the smallpox, the settlers. Empire. Capitalism. Someone's going to survive this. My grandfathers and grandmothers lived right here, in this valley, and they didn't just live, they were fucking heroes. And there's no way I'm leaving this place, not to move to James Bay and dig up rare earth metals so some corporate asshole can have his new tech and talk big and stupid about how he's going to save the world. I'm not going to rebuild Ontario. I'm making this place into something new. And to do that, we need copper."

Then — without waiting for Kit to speak or join him — he stood and turned again to the dark interior of the house and began his search.

Kit's eyes prickled and he gripped the pencil he held awkwardly, because how often did he use a pencil? Under his hand, the list of things they'd found in the last house:

Estimates of copper wire, and available glass. Old computer equipment, containing rare earth metals that might be recovered. Catalytic converters in old garages, with the atom-thick film of palladium. So much junk. So much useless junk.

The problem with the burn was that you had to do it in the rainy season, for obvious reasons, and Kit was never entirely dry, nor properly warm for the whole month of October he spent in the bush, which coincided with his eighteenth birthday and seemed deeply unfair. Even when they were under cover it was filthy weather, a steady drizzle that occasionally intensified into heavy rain, but never stopped. Once he got excited because the sky looked faintly blue over the bay, and Trish thought she saw a splash of sunset on the interior mountains. That lasted like an hour and then they were again crouching around a fire in the backyard of the house in which they were staying. None of it dried him out nor warmed him up.

"Can we light it inside?" he'd asked. "There's a fireplace."

Benno had given him the don't be a fucking idiot look and he'd subsided, brooding, then listened to Benno lecture them all on the area they were surveying for the more skilled salvage parties that followed after, and the demolitions group who'd burn it all down. These hillsides were perfect for Garry oak and forest gardens full of bitter cherry and crabapple. The bay below them hosted oyster beds. The salmon were running again up Koksilah, since the Douglas firs had begun their return and shaded the riverbed so the fry wouldn't cook on their way back to the open ocean.

Across the fire, Trish listened with her chin on her hands, thinking thoughts inaccessible to Kit. Her eyes were warmly brown and her hair was dark and shiny and he wanted —

Just a month ago there had been a window between Milton and whoever she'd been into before. Stephanie, probably. She'd been with Steph for like a year. He'd kissed her. Or she'd kissed him. He couldn't shake that memory. End of summer, on the beach, September twilight and a fire. They were drinking terrible spruce beer and someone was singing and playing an old guitar; they were skipping rocks, wrestling, all the bullshit kids do when there's nothing to do. She'd tucked herself under his arm, leaning against a log at the high-tide line, and he'd never recovered from that, how it had felt. How warm she was, and how in the chill of 3 a.m., when the tide had overtaken their fire, his butt was numb from sitting but he couldn't stand moving away from her, not for the brief, miraculous hours of her closeness, smelling like smoke and salt water.

Benno kept sending them out together because he was an asshole.

They left at dawn and walked north along the route he'd given them, following what remained of the streets paved a hundred years before. According to the old maps it should be a cul-de-sac at the end of a marginal neighborhood, south-facing, on the shoulder of a hill, established in the 1990s and abandoned before Kit was born, when anyone with money left the smoking crap-heap that was left of the island.

It was mid-morning when they arrived and they went door to door in what had been a rich white dude's neighborhood. He was tired, and sulky, and Trish reciprocated with silence, interrupted only by terse and necessary words. Until now.

"Hey," she said, her voice warm with surprise. "That's camas."

The most words she'd said to him that day. Goddamn camas. I bet you and Milty gathered goddamn camas together, skipping around like a couple of fucking bunny rabbits. I bet you dug a pit and steamed it on the beach and fed him. I bet he licked your fingers. Fucker.

Chunks of asphalt underfoot and Kit thought again about what the world must have been like before, swathed in streets and houses, green grass cut by kids with lawnmowers, like they saw sometimes on old DVDs. You could still see the shape the houses had left behind, the curbs and foundations, and they felt as unreal as anything else he saw on screen. Like, when he was little and watched movies at the library Benno's granddad ran — *Star Wars, Big Trouble in Little China, Friends* — he couldn't tell the difference between cities and starships, and he'd asked his Grandma if she'd lived on a battlecruiser, or flown a tie-fighter, or gone to Central Perk. There had been lasers and sugar and wookies in the old world, right? She'd laughed and laughed and cried a tiny bit and said no, none of those things, those were all just stories. She'd grown up right here in the valley, but it was different back then. Lit up at night, zooming with cars — she made the noises, because they were so rare in the neighborhood he couldn't always remember.

She remembered flying down to San Francisco when she was twenty, spending the night out walking through the rain during Nuit Blanche — the whole city a candle burning, full of contortionists and masks and LEDs. A dream city, above the ocean. She'd danced all night with a girl she'd loved, glitter falling from their hair as they ran down the steep streets toward the ocean.

He remembered understanding the words, but not really. She'd touched his head, hugged him and said, again, "It's hard to explain."

"What's an LED? What's a contortionist?"

73

He kept asking. What's San Francisco? What's nuit blanche? The questions were infinite, each word she said open-ing up a whole other world, more alien with each explanation.

When they used the spotty satellite link at the library to hear the news, he saw bits of the other world, cities and crowds and concerts and coffee and a new Mars mission, somewhere far away from this rainy corner of nowhere, where his only future was in undoing what had been done by generations who'd lived brief golden lives, sucking all the sweetness from the world before he was even born.

"But it's camas," Trish said again.

Startled, he looked at the ground where she crouched and saw the leaves she was examining. Then his habitual, willful crankiness overtook his surprise, and he said, "Can we just do the walk through and move on?"

"But that's good — that means we can do something here. Don't you pay attention to — never mind."

Here she walked down the middle of what had once been one of those ridiculous suburban streets you saw in old movies, so wide you could grow a whole family's potatoes in the land they paved over.

"Salal," Trish said. "Oregon grape."

"That's everywhere."

"Are you sure we're in the right area? Where are the houses?"

They followed the curve of the street — visible only as a flat space covered in branches and fallen leaves — and he saw what she meant. Everywhere they went the old world was burnt out and overgrown, all ash and parking lots. Here, though, a deer path led them to the last cul-de-sac and ahead of them the darkness opened into a meadow edged by Douglas fir. In August, Kit thought, it would be brilliant with heat waves, pale gold and olive green, the sky overhead an arresting blue. He could almost smell the heat and the earth underfoot.

"Wild ginger," Trish said again, kneeling to touch the dull winter leaves, her hands wet with rain. "And there are at least a dozen crab apples. Orchard apples as well. And a plum. Bitter cherry."

Deer droppings underfoot and in the trees, a richness of birdsong. By some miracle, the usual invaders — scotch broom, English ivy — were absent, despite the open ground.

"It'll need another burn," she said. "In the next year or two."

"What? Yeah, we're going to —"

But that wasn't what she meant, and Kit could see her thoughts at work, its restless imagination propelling her into the future, and he realized how much Trish resembled Benno.

She reached up to pick an apple, one of those orphans still hanging on the leafless branch, though it was October. Its russet skin struck by the watery sunlight that reached between the cloud cover and the horizon, illuminating every leaf, every droplet, the grass underfoot suddenly arcing fire. She bit into the fruit and said, "you could live here, you know. Town isn't too far, so you'd still see people. You could probably grow potatoes lower down the slope, too, if you terraced it."

Kit swallowed. He saw that future, like the sun had opened a window in time as well as cloud cover. He saw the open grasses burnt back to make way for the winter-dormant roots of camas, and the deep-rooted Garry oak trees that thrived beneath the soil. He heard Trish's voice saying, *here, we dig here* as together they built stone walls and terraced the lower hillside. He saw the purple blooms of wild onion and garlic raising their heads in one of Benno's savannas, the rare and unnatural ecosystem maintained only by fire. It was — Benno said it in a way that Kit only now understood what had before seemed like babble — a collaboration between who we used to be, before settlement, and who we're going to become.

But we're always a collaboration, Benno had tried to tell him: there's nothing we don't touch, nothing that isn't changed by our feet on the soil and our hands reaching into the new, soft needles of Douglas fir in springtime. We have a heavy step,

Benno said, not just the old settlers, but us too. The best we can do is hope that our footprints don't break anyone's heart.

A long time ago this was forest. Then it was a forest garden. Then it was concrete and glass and the pages of old *Readers Digest* magazines. It was car exhaust and hula hoops and Kool-Aid stands and birthday parties and hotdogs and CD changers in the backs of cars playing *Big Shiny Tunes 3*. Now it was something new, maybe with an actual future.

They climbed together to the top of the meadow, a long slope up the hillside, until the ground grew too steep for houses.

"When do you think it burned?" he asked.

"I don't know. Those firs are fifty at least. And look —"

They had reached what Kit thought was an arbutus, but which he now saw wasn't exactly the familiar red-barked tree. This one was gold and it was strangely shaped, its branches turned at right angles, growing parallel with the ground. And not just one tree, he realized, but several.

"Inosculation," Trish said.

"What?"

She knelt and pointed out the trunks, "Four trees fused at branch and trunk. No — six. Mason does it for fencing out at Kaatza."

Kit walked around it. "Awesome," he said as he sat.

"Don't — it's —"

"— It's a bench. Someone grew a bench." He traced the living joinery with his hand, seeing where someone had bent the trunks of infant arbutus around one another, had trained the branches upward and over some now-lost frame to form the back of a seat. He laughed at the ingenuity and beauty and ridiculousness. "Come on," he said. "Sit down."

He slid over and made room on the living bench. She joined him, and together they looked down the hillside toward the bay. Around them, branches of a tree neither Kit nor Trish could name seemed to toss the sunlight back out to the sky.

"What is it?" Kit asked, touching the tree's golden skin.

"Arbutus, I guess. But I've never seen one like it. Not that color."

"I thought you were the genius."

She looked away and he thought, she's going to call me a dick and that's it, the moment's gone. He blushed, ashamed of how shallow his words were, how slight in the face of this sudden illumination. He wanted to say something true to her, something commensurate with her strength and beauty and breathtaking single-mindedness.

He said, "I'm sorry. It's really beautiful."

This time, she nodded.

Pub Food

Every year or two, Kaatza still got government food from Saskatchewan: wheat, garbanzos, canola oil. It wasn't as reliable as it had been five years before, and you had to go to Nanaimo and camp out on the dock, where it arrived in one of the few still-operating coastguard vessels. But the food had saved them after a droughty summer and a bad winter when they'd dug stunted potatoes from the earth and the cougars had hunted the deer before they could.

Garbanzos meant falafel, and she could make flatbread. Or she could save eggs and make brioche, but it would be better if she could get yeast instead of their usual sourdough. In town, Sophie asked Benno and a couple of other people about yeast, but no one had anything. "Any luck with the other stuff?" Benno asked, circumspect.

"No. Maybe. Who knows."

She'd gone to Nanaimo with a kilo of her best. No one was holding. Supplies from Vancouver and Seattle had dried up. Somewhere Fentanyl and Oxy must still exist. Somewhere there were still addicts and big pharma and chemotherapy and all that horror, but not here, not for them. That made it harder in a way she had not expected: a grinding, rageful resentment growing each time she looked at Jake and thought, if we lived a few hundred k to the south or east, would he be in a hospital by now? If he had been born earlier, or later? She'd been growing *Papaver somniferum* for when the painkillers dried up, but she'd had more luck with *Lactusa virosa*. Poor Man's opium. A sedative.

Okay, but she could approximate the tortilla chips, and then nachos. Guacamole was impossible, obviously, but black bean dip, maybe? She had cilantro, cumin, and chilis. Sour cream in small quantities. She'd considered hummus — given the garbanzos — but sesame seeds were a problem. She knew of at least one place on Saanich peninsula growing them in a rare, hot corner, but not so many that one could call it production. Her own experiments had produced a stunted row of them the year before, mildewed in the ground. She'd need lemons, too, though she had raised one in the glass house, nurturing it through a stormy winter, while inside Jacob sat in a chair at the window, staring out at the firewood he could no longer cut, the wood box he could no longer fill, and grew quieter with each month.

For the rest of that week she dug and weeded and thought. She'd read in one of their old books that Paclitaxel — an old chemotherapy drug — was extracted from Pacific yew trees, and she'd surveyed the nearby woods, even bringing in some green twigs, but Jake, asking what she was doing had refused absolutely: "Soph, I'm not drinking tea made out of yew needles."

"It's not tea," she'd said defensively. "It would probably be a tincture."

His denial hadn't stopped her from doing more research, but while they had a room full of old library books Benno had collected, it was first aid more than pharmaceuticals. The satellite link was spotty that spring — solar flares, or some accelerating collapse, they couldn't tell — but she stared restlessly at the planet icon on her phone, the glowing dots that circled and circled and circled and never connected.

She could at least make something painfully sweet, now that they had a quarter acre of sugar beets, which yielded fodder for Raj's growing herd, and a coarse, pale brown sugar. Or, as Mason had put it that first year, a sugar-like substance. Not that it had stopped him from dropping a scant teaspoon into a glass of mint tea and — for a moment — smiling. For weeks the house had smelled richly of molasses. When the littlest kids in town came to visit, Sophie scooped out teaspoons of pale brown crystals just for the pleasure of watching their faces transformed, squealing with delight. It was the reason Auntie Soph was so popular these days.

This problem of pub food and birthday cakes had been troubling her for six weeks, ever since the night when Jake couldn't sleep and they sat awake together, talking and smoking Nepenthe. He told her, suddenly, about the birthday cake that Grandma had made for him, when he and Mason arrived here, newly orphaned by wildfires and influenza.

"It was all full of sprinkles, mountains of icing. She said I could eat as much as I wanted, and I swear I ate half of it. Then I threw it up, and my puke was rainbow. Well, at first. Then it turned purple. But goddamn that was good."

He laughed. Coughed. Laughed.

"Funfetti cake. I wonder if those still exist."

"Somewhere, I bet."

"What about nachos? The kind we used to get in pubs. Cheese and pickled jalapenos and hunks of steak. God I miss guacamole. I wonder how many avocado trees have survived?"

"Cheddar cheese," she said. "The sharp stuff from Tillamook."

She wondered if Tillamook was still there, or if some combination of fire and drought and flood had excised it from the coast, and with it the dairy and the cheddar cheese and the ice cream. The thought was newly horrible, though it should be familiar. She realized that she had a largely unexamined hope that far to the south on the Oregon coast, kids were eating vanilla soft serve at Tillamook dairy.

For years they had silently agreed not to talk about what they missed in the old world, but then the doctor at Duncan's temporary clinic confirmed the diagnosis they had already suspected and after that why bother pretending they didn't miss ice cream and guacamole.

It was early spring and so much work to do, but he'd insisted on taking days away from work to take them from Kaatza to the clinic in town and a real doctor. They had a load of potatoes in Raj's wagon and two old horses to pull it. A couple of kilos of weed and a few nuggets of opium latex to trade, and requests from half the people at Kaatza for acetaminophen, books, shoes, wire.

They waited a whole day to see the doctor, hanging around the park near the old rail line where a guy with a guitar sung old songs. Jacob sat up so he could watch, leaning against the bag of old clothes they'd swapped for potatoes.

"I feel like it's changed," Jacob said when the man played "It's All Still Fine," crooning through the bridge. "Like there's an extra verse. The bit about a fire burning in your heart forever."

"I don't remember that. I used to sing it constantly when I was twelve. Like, at the absolute top of my lungs in the car with Dad. He said he hated it but he totally knew all the words."

Jake laughed. Coughed again.

It took them four days to get into town, see the doctor, and get home again. Four days away from the dairy herds, the firebreaks, the traplines, the garden. Four days to get a twenty-minute meeting that confirmed what they all suspected. On the slow road home, they didn't talk much, but her brain raced into the near future: pain management; whether they should try the doctor in Nanaimo; how they'd move his bed into the front room, where he'd have a view of the lake.

Poutine? She thought of collecting the oil, then how many armloads of wood to heat it to 325 degrees? When she was younger and cleverer, she might have calculated the calories burned to raise oil to the necessary temperature and hold it there for the time it took to cook a strip of potato. Not anymore: she was too tired.

Benno knew about her plans, though she guessed what he really thought of all this desperate activity in search of cake and cheeseburgers. Not that he was judgmental, of course. He went through old cookbooks and brought her what he found: that you could make your own aquafaba from garbanzos, something like whipped cream or meringue, that rosewater could be used in place of vanilla. Rosewater and elderflower, maybe. It wouldn't be a Funfetti cake with a mountain of icing so sweet you puked your birthday guts out. But it could be a little bit of joy among the government wheat-and-garbanzo ration and the potato-fueled winter, or puddings made of stinging nettles and venison boiled together in an old pillowcase. In February, when the rain fell without remission, and the days were short and dark and you were soaked through half the time looking after the chickens and goats, you craved some richness. Anything. The crisp resistance of bacon. Butter and eggs. She could pound the beet sugar fine. She'd replace the recipe's milk with rosewater. Then whipped cream tinted pink with beet juice.

Ginger. Rose. Mint. No sprinkles. No fentanyl. No paclitaxel even if they were surrounded by yew trees. No silver dragées. No antibiotics for the cough that got steadily worse, his skin hot and his green sputum luridly streaked with red.

In the afternoon she picked an armful of wild roses and a dozen more from the apricot climber that covered half of the house — the one Jake's grandmother, Maureen, had planted long before Jake and Mason were born. Maureen had also planted the fruit trees, and built the first garden walls, which

Sophie had been extending for decades now. She'd started the slow work converting stony soil into good earth among mountains full of rain and shadow. The dazzle from the lake, she'd told Mason, accelerated the growth of tomatoes. But Maureen hadn't reckoned on 2°C by mid-century and with it the wildfires, the drought, the floods and desettlement.

Nevertheless, Maureen's apricot roses flourished. Sophie dumped the fragrant bucket into a pot on the woodstove, simmered it, then strained and decanted the pale pinkish liquid. It would keep in a refrigerator, but their batteries had been dying for the last year and lighting had priority, especially during the long nights of Jake's fever.

The kitchen smelled of summer, leafy and resinous, the way the woods smelled when they were dry and brilliant in June. But she couldn't shake the memory of how birthday cakes used to be, brilliant pink icing and sugar roses and she felt the tears, and she had to sit for a while in the pantry, among the barrels and hanging bunches, the bags of government wheat. In the walls, the skitter of mice going about their hidden lives.

In the bedroom, Jake was coughing in his sleep. Then he was quiet and she listened hard to his silence and thought — as she often had in the last week — is this it? Is this it?

She breathed in. She breathed out. She left the pantry and walked the dark rose-scented hallway to the room that had been his grandmother's, long before Sophie's time.

He was so still she thought, this must be it, this must, and I'm too late, and I should have stoked the stove with all their winter wood to heat the oil and make him french fries. His hands were cold. She slid into bed beside him, and as she curled into his back, her eyes burned and prickled and spilled. He moved in her arms and his sleepy, torn voice said, "you smell like roses," before he fell into a deep and terrible sleep.

The Cathedral Arboreal

In August 2100, Kit told Sophie about the impending arrival of the Canadians, how she was invited down island to the Cathedral Arboreal to meet with them. It wasn't just them, either. They were bringing a violinist who'd play in the Cathedral. It would be recorded. They were going to interview folks, too. Something about historians back in Canada wanting a record about what it's been like.

But, he insisted, not only that. It had been a brilliant summer. The oyster beds were rich in Cowichan Bay. Chinook would be running upriver and the gardens were the richest Trish had ever seen. Kit promised barbecues on the beach, potatoes baked in the sand and maybe a lamb roasted the way she liked it, with oregano, rosemary, and garlic. More important than all that, though, was the concert in the Cathedral, which still didn't have a roof, so it would be open to the stars and the breeze off the bay, even if the weather was hot. Dad wanted her approval on the new garden they'd start clearing when the potatoes and apples were in, south-facing toward the water. She'd meet a couple of new babies who'd just arrived that year. There'd been weddings since she'd last visited. The long, warm evenings were perfect, he said, for a party. For several parties.

No no no. It wasn't Kit who told her about the trip. It was Louis. Kit's oldest boy looked uncannily like Kit had when he arrived at Kaatza thirty years before, skinny and tall, a glutton for work and for every fragment of knowledge she bothered to impart. Embarrassing that she was so unstuck in time, making grandmotherly mistakes. Sometimes a string of names came out of her mouth when she shouted for someone: Jake-Mason-Benno-Kit before she landed on the right one. Louis.

"It'll be next month," he said. "They're in Vancouver now."

"Why?"

"They want to know what's going on out here, Dad said."

"That's fine. But they don't need me."

She remembered Louis as a toddler on Kit's shoulders, then — confusedly — as a skinny kid sullenly digging trenches for the potatoes. Then he was a young father walking little Meg through the carrots. All Kit and Trish's kids had stayed with her and learned the gardener's trade, but Louis had remained, her official grandson, Meg her official great granddaughter, along with a dozen others around town, running in and out of the house as their parents worked and they learned the principles of gardening, its rhythms, its disappointments. Jake would have known all their names without guessing or having to call out *you in the black shirt* —

"They're going to send a jeep."

"There'll be another slide on the highway."

"They cleared the last one. And Dad says the Empress trees have fixed the hillsides all the way to Victoria."

"Take the river. Go as far as Skutz falls by canoe, then walk into town."

Louis wasn't listening. His father had been the same way when he got an idea, overshooting all of them, and halfway gone before anyone knew what he had planned. It was Kit who realized the possibilities of the aurum, for grafting, for growing what could only be called living buildings. She remembered the light on his face when Mason showed him that book, how he'd asked about McPherson Library when he saw the stamp

85

on the flyleaf. It was only a matter of time before he headed down island where the university endured, its nurseries and gardens expanding from the old campus all the way down to the tideline, over land once devoted to pink condominiums and neo-Tudor cottages. He'd learned what he needed from Mason, from her, from the Arborists in Victoria. Now he was building — no, growing — the Cathedral Arboreal overlooking Cowichan Bay, in what had once been a suburban cul-de-sac.

"Kit," she muttered, the name emerging unbidden, as so often she muttered *Jacob* under her breath. Often when she was thinking, she heard her voice before she realized she was speaking out loud: *Jacob, what were we thinking putting the aspen break so close to town, they're going to need more space.* Or *What do you think about making the nursery into a real school? Bringing more kids down from Nanaimo while I still remember anything worth teaching?*

Sometimes she just said his name, like a prayer or an epithet. *Jake.*

Louis didn't seem to notice. He brought a tablet she didn't remember, something new-looking, and showed her the invitation, "Come on, Grandma. We're going to go." Then his smile, cheeky and persuasive, ready to wheedle her into good spirits.

"How did you hear?"

"The High Web. The Noosphere. It's the new satellite network. We talk to Mom and Dad all the time now. Meg sees cartoons from Wellington, even."

"High what?"

"I got a letter. Passenger pigeon. Smoke signals. You'll want to hear the rest, though. The folks coming out from Canada have brought meds."

This meant something. "For Meg? You think?"

Louis' little girl, Meg, had bad lungs, congested every winter, wheezing through the hot months, a constant worry.

"There's a chance," he said. "Who knows. But there's a chance."

She must have fallen asleep because she woke in the darkness and said "Jacob?" His presence so real, she could be twenty and sitting beside him on Sombrio Beach on the day they'd met. Reaching down to the cooler for a beer and — accidentally, maybe on purpose — brushing her fingers across his hand in the darkness. Soph, he'd said, Soph, and then taken her hand and the accident wasn't an accident anymore and then the bodyrush and everything was beautiful.

"Jacob?" At the open window, the song of a new bird with a chirrup like a cellphone. She fumbled under her pillow instinctively, because though it had been decades since she'd had a phone that worked, the action was still automatic, like her hand didn't know time had passed.

"I won't go," she said again.

Louis sat up in the chair beside her bed. "What?"

"Where would I even stay? I can't sleep in a tent."

"Mom and Dad are giving you their cottage. Just think, though, a real concert with real musicians. It'll be in the evening."

"I'm too old to travel."

"Sunset in the Cathedral is something else. You should see it. The walls are all arches with screens of crossed branches that throw these crazy shadows across the floor. And it's all gold because of the aurum. Dad says it's growing so fast they'll have the second storey done in a few years, and then work on crossing the branches for the roof."

"I know it's on a hill."

"I've heard they want to do an oral history of the — what do you like to call it? Dark Age?"

"Then they can come here. Is the Dark Age over?"

That evening, Louis' girlfriend Jenny sat with her, rocking their youngest, who was colicky, while Meg played with blocks on the floor. The windows were open to catch the late evening breeze and with it the scent of wood roses from the garden, and the resinous sweet of the grand spruce near the house, its long trunks newly cut that afternoon, in their tenth year of growth.

Daisuigi, Mason had called it. He and Jake had started a dozen of them around town, a fast-growing modified species, some remnant of an experiment they'd found down-island. The spruce had been changed, but nevertheless held onto its sweet scent and the sticky, brightly burning sap of the original tree. She was grateful for that sweetness. Not all things had to be lost.

Once, a long time ago, she'd been a kid in an over-heated bedroom, dreaming of silence and cold water and wilderness and now she was an old woman and the street on which she had dreamed was probably inundated by king tides or green with the spill of flooding rivers. Maybe there were new wetlands along Westminster Avenue, where she had often walked to the 7-Eleven. Mussels growing over the old Starbucks on the corner and ducks diving into the shallow waters of the expanding Fraser River, all the arable land of Delta salt-soaked, killing the black soil that accumulated over thousands of years. The strawberry fields, the masses of dahlias and chrysanthemums.

She wondered how she'd fallen in love with forests at all, considering they'd just been the skyline for much of her childhood, the smoke-whitened haze of Lynn Valley and Cypress looming to the north, streaked with ash.

But there had been the patch of grass out behind the townhouse in Ladner, a couple of cedars along the sidewalk, dying in the heat. Dad had old Canadian Tire buckets from which miraculous strawberries dropped, and in others he grew cherry tomatoes. The first seeds she'd ever planted had been a packet of marigolds he bought her from the dollar store. Some hot night in a too-short spring, when the ding-ding-ding from the walk signal on the corner punctured her sleep, her bedroom ceiling painted red by traffic lights. But in the egg carton little green curls pushed up through the soil and then — precious and secret — the first leaves unfurling. Frilled orange and yellow flowers she and Dad had transplanted into plastic buckets and set on the step outside their front door. Those flowers had glowed and bloomed all summer and into the winter and she had been so proud.

She was surprised to find she missed the streetlights, the sound of the walk signal. Not far away, the Pacific roared on, seeming not to notice the crumbling human world. On winter nights the rain was incessant and the darkness absolute, but she remembered crowds and the smell of hot fryer fat on summer evenings, the sky glowing amber long after midnight. Being seventeen, with a vodka buzz just before dawn while the wildfire smoke filled her lungs. She'd never been hungry because there was nacho cheese from the spigot at the 7-11 or shawarma or roti. Green patent high heels in a shop window. A new lipstick in purple and teal multichrome. For so long she had endeavored to contain them, but the memories were still inside her, as her body weakened and her mind fractured. Pushing up through the soil.

Did kids still congregate under streetlights while fires burned across the inlet? What about in Sacramento or Portland? There had been periodic burns all the previous summer, but the breaks had held around the valley, and the new aurum stands resisted fire even better than aspen colonies did. The interior mountains of the island were now teaming with gold leaves. She'd had a load of Empress trees, the sterile varietal with a few extra fungal-resistant genes that grew so fast she thought she could see them move. In a few centuries they might claw enough carbon back from the atmosphere to drop them back to 2°C over pre-industrial temperatures. Or not.

But, somewhere in the world, did kids stand under streetlights at dusk, slapping mosquitoes and watching desultory pickup games on the soccer field? The kids here didn't. They ran for the secret campgrounds, hiking away from the lake to fuck unsteathily in the woods, buzzed on the spruce beer someone was brewing haphazardly in town. As they should, she told herself, but wanted to know that some kid, somewhere, drank lychee and rose bubble tea while walking downtown in ridiculous shoes, eyelids glittering purple and silver. Staring through brilliant glass windows at the wonder of a restaurant where people in linen drank wine. That the city wasn't dead, just smaller than it had been, and ready to be revived when the world stopped ending.

Kit had never been off the island. He was just a teenager when Benno brought him out to work with Mason, decades ago now. He'd been born working, could run a trapline and dress the rabbits he caught and cook them — badly — over a fire. But he was also restless for stories, for ideas, for the books that Benno gave him. He and Trish had three kids by the time they were twenty-five. He was a grandfather now. Which made her so many generations removed from the littlest kids, she might as well be an alien, an antique goddess. A relict.

The problem was she couldn't control these wandering thoughts, especially at night. She seemed to travel backward in time, from her years with Jake, to her childhood, to earlier days even than that. She wasn't exactly asleep, but she could hear her own deep breaths as she saw, behind her eyelids, a young woman in 1984 — how did she know the year? — at a gas station. Then she recognized the photograph: her grandmother, twenty, the hose and nozzle in her right hand, her sunglasses sliding down her face, her black hair enormous and her jeans tight. She was smiling at someone. Not Sophie's grandfather.

Her boyfriend's getting a Slurpee inside while she fills the tank of their van. The concrete glazed with oil, chewing gum, echoing with the slap of flip-flops. She closes her eyes while the tank fills and the volatile air around her seems to shimmer with heat and gasoline. The world is brilliant with possibility and speed and distance, tinted orange by the haze over Vancouver as they descend to sea-level, before they turn south and barrel through Peace Arch crossing. The names ticking past them: Bellingham, Seattle, Tacoma. 101 through Oregon, then California. Arcata. Eureka. Fortuna. And she's driving and there's nothing — nothing — to her right but the Pacific and she hits the accelerator. He's passed out on the sleeping bags in the back, and she could drive all night like this, the empty road and the stars, but she pulls over at a rest stop, vibrating with eight hours behind the wheel, the redwoods rising to the south and east and she thinks, this is the most beautiful thing in the world, the engine under the hood ticking as it cools, and a tank full of gas. Mendocino. Gualala. Bodega Bay.

A hundred years ago the world was huge and rich and full, like nighttime in California. It smelled like benzene.

The next morning Sophie woke rested, her mind quiet, and it seemed the scent of gasoline was still with her, and with it the lost pleasure of acceleration. She went to the window to watch the lake glow into daylight. Louis was outside, a shovel over his shoulder. There were sounds of breakfast in the kitchen.

When she joined them, she said, without preamble: "We'll go."

Louis just nodded. He knew her well enough not to crow his victory.

The Canadians arrived in September 2100.

To Kit they seemed absurdly young, a bunch of twenty-five-year-old adventurers in grey bioplastic gear, anti-microbial and self-healing, who had set out from Toronto the previous spring. They arrived at the old government dock in a tender from an American coastguard ship drifting off the bay. "It's so *clean*," Trish said when it arrived in the twilight, where the village had gathered to observe this curious, official invasion.

"It's like something from before," Sarwan said. He worked in the nursery with the antique CRISPR-6, producing high-protein potatoes and sterile Empress trees that grew at a reckless and unnatural seven meters a year.

"How many of them are there? Does anyone know?"

"Fourteen, they said. I think they left some behind in Seattle. And then the other mainlanders. The musician."

"Who's cooking this week? Should we put someone else in the kitchen?"

"It's been a good summer," Sarwan said. He was right: the river was already crowded with Chinook, more than anyone could eat, not even the bears and the ravens far up the Koksilah and Cowichan Rivers. The oyster beds overflowed, the ocean gardens purple with mussels, and the apples heavy on their branches.

"There'll be more than enough to eat," Kit finally said. "Maybe they brought some books."

Trish, eyes still fixed on the ship, nodded. "I'd like some new books, and if they brought meds I'll give them all the salmon they can carry."

"It's *spectacular*," Khush said the first morning, as they walked together from the largest longhouse, where the Corps were housed for the duration, to the nursery. That's what they called themselves: the Corps, of either Engineers or Diplomats, depending on who you talked to. Khush was the young man assigned to Kit for — whatever it was they were supposed to be doing. Something about exchange, networks, insight into local land management tech. "I mean, I saw pictures, but it's like *WHAT?* in person. And this morning we went swimming. No algae blooms, though we're surprised you aren't using more algaltech." The young man shook his head in wonder. He wore new clothes, travel-worn, but nothing inherited from an uncle, his boots unmended, some tough man-made material shaped neatly to his foot, and flexible.

"Where's the bioplastic from?" Kit asked.

"Oh. Like, algae and some soybean. With a matrix of nanocellulose from a black willow we're growing in Sowesto. We actually brought some with us for you. They'll do super great out in that estuary." He pointed up Cowichan Bay, where the rivers spread into wetlands.

Khush always spoke in first person plural, so an image formed in Kit's mind of this huge smiling crowd that occupied all of Ontario, millions moving in unison, their eyes fixed on a brilliant future, children raised in those efficient government-built habitats he'd seen in the Noosphere, tending the willows on the river every afternoon. They all talked about the riparian microclimates and carbon uptake, hours of sunlight and water systems and algae. They talked about Detroit and Cincinnati, the hubs of American innovation, where they'd gone on eight week study rotations when they were teenagers.

He took Khush over to the nursery, where Sarwan's five hundred sterile Empresses were ready for transplant on rocky hillsides up the Malahat, to secure against erosion and protect the new, tenuous thread of highway they'd so recently recovered from landslides.

"What's the uptake?"

Kit must have looked like "huh?" because Khush clarified: "Just ballpark."

"I have no idea, dude."

As they walked back to the longhouse to eat, Kit looked down at the keloid scar that ran from his right wrist to the elbow, showing below his torn cuff. That was from when he was still out at Kaatza, working with Mason, and had fallen off the roof of the greenhouse where they were whitewashing the panes against the blistering June sunshine. It was crooked, like a pleat in his skin, though Sophie had stitched him up neatly after giving him a couple of shots of painfully raw potato vodka. Khush's skin was clear of scars.

They were all so *happy*, Trish said that afternoon. Cheerfully pursuing every possible abatement protocol: mycorrhizal carbon sinks and deep-rooted genetically mod-ified grasses rolling over the flat, green farmland of Sowesto. The consistent, measurable sequestration of carbon from the choked atmosphere, by way of a hundred thousand rational-ized protocols. They'd turned Lake Ontario's warm algae blooms into biodiesel and livestock feed, a massive, carbon-negative system farming the lakes. Sure, the fish were all dead, and you came out slimy if you tried to swim, but that was the cost of recovery. The Detroit River was thick and green with a new species — "lipid count is *astronomical!*" Khush said — built to consume the toxic sediments that still lined its bed, and fueling transit systems on both sides of the border.

"You ever thought of going to Ontario?" Khush asked as Kit took him through the cathedral after lunch, to the north-west corner and the vestibule he'd tended for the last months, where the intertwining branches of the aurum crossed in diamonds. He was prouder of this than he was of anything other than the meadow he and Trish maintained up the hill, which had emerged richly green from the previous winter's burn.

"Never."

It wasn't true. Ask him forty years before and he would have said yes. Yes, anywhere but here, yes to a place where things were happening, and the streets lit at night, where the darkness was not absolute, and the world steadily shrinking away from him, no matter how much he drank, or how angry he got.

"You ever been off Vancouver Island?"

"Nope."

"We're doing the same stuff as you but on, like, a larger scale." He looked over the coppiced elderberries that fenced the potato fields and said, "We're sequestering 100,000 tons of carbon a year. Just my unit."

"You're in a unit?"

"Yeah, I'm London Riding. Back in the fifties? My parents were relocated there from Toronto. And because of our output? We're looking at a new biorefinery, for the willows. Just the ones on the Thames."

"We're going to try to extend the eastern vestibule. And we dug a new potato field this summer."

"Cool. What are you taking up? Like, a rough guess?"

Kit stared at him. Again. "You should talk to Sarwan. He can do math."

"When we're working, we think about it. You know, what's locked away each second. For our kids. You got any kids?"

"Three. Two grandkids."

"Okay. Wow. You know, we're going to be taking it all back. Bringing you home. I bet your grandkids will come to Detroit for training. I totally bet that. Detroit is awesome. I was at this party once? And —" Khush went on, but Kit wasn't listening much.

That first evening, the Corps demonstrated new tech: water filtration and bioplastic tents and sleeping bags. They talked about supply chains: the Pacific routes, the Panama Canal re-opened. The Suez Canal cleared of wrecks and mines. How they'd re-establish high speed rail through the Rockies following the old imperial routes. Multigenerational projects. Fifty-year plans fueled by a hundred million human hearts beating in unified zeal.

Though the Corps was unfailingly polite, they clearly liked some things better than others: not the reggae band, but the smoked salmon; not the kids' slapstick skits on the beach after supper, but definitely the abundant weed grown in a sunny corner of the main kitchen garden.

Khush particularly liked the living bridge Kit had begun building across a narrow, seasonal creek not far from the village. He tried to explain what Mason had first seen in the roots of the aurum: their voraciousness and flexibility, the way they crossed rocky territory, winding between the stones, under moss and over the silvery quartz diorite of the inlet. He tried to tell Khush about its beauty, its endurance and suitability for grafting and inosculation, how up the coast they were growing Daisugi aurum forests as firebreaks around the farms. How they had firewood and building materials every few years from that generous and adaptable tree. He was planning to begin an orchard that winter, for Meg when she'd grown up, the aurum forming its walls. Trish had begun ocean gardens for the kids too, where one day they'd cultivate mussels and oysters.

And sure, Khush was effusive about the bridge, which was still mostly just a frame of poles and cross-pieces Kit had lashed together with cedar rope. Back at the long house, Khush shouted, "Guys, guys, you gotta see this!" and described the roots feeling their way out from the banks, which Kit had started to interweave where they met in the middle. "A living bridge, using that yellow tree. It looks like it's got some banyan inserts, maybe? Does anyone know what they were working on in genetic forestry around here?"

He wanted to stop Khush and say, *Look! Look*! At the luminous roots reaching out into space. He'd seen the possibility thirty years before, when he sat on a bench some arborist had grown into the hillside above Cowichan Bay, a vision that had resolved further when, decades ago, he had sat at Sophie's kitchen table looking through an old book from their library, its back cover gone, but its pages full of collaborations between tree and human: living bridges, leafy walls, branching towers. That had been the moment the cathedral flickered into being, though it remained nascent for years, his vision of an animate building, its roof full of birdsong.

The Canadians had brought two musicians with them, part of the recording project funded by a distant billionaire with some connection to the Salish sea. Her name was Belinda. She traveled with her son and accompanist, a kid who was never without this collapsible electronic keyboard on which he noodled compulsively. Often, Kit heard them playing together, a high, angelic sound that unsettled him, though he recognized its beauty, that the scales and arpeggios progressed with supernatural perfection and the melodies were entrancing. But each rehearsal left him feeling something like heartbreak, and that pain was unsustainable when he had so much to do. When the sounds carried from the houses on the shore, he fled them, walking further inland to the cathedral and the nursery, then up to their meadow to pick apples with the birds and the singing grasshoppers. He'd sit on the old, still-living bench and wait until he was sure they were done. At night, when Belinda joined the evening fire on the beach, Trish spoke with her, laughing, and Kit sat at the far edge of the firelight.

"The violin was her mom's. It has a name. Nepenthe, like the weed Sophie grows," she reported back. "I didn't know you named violins."

She was watching him closely, but he only nodded, looking down the slope to the fire's embers, where the kids — Canadians and Cathedralists — were singing: *where does that river run, poor boy?* Kit's memories already slingshotting back to Mason, who rarely broke his silence except to talk about music: concert halls and theaters and crowds listening in silence, or struggling in sweaty moshpits, or dancing outside at

Jericho Beach before the rising tides destroyed the beach there. Crowds of them high as fuck, thoughtless, young.

"You okay?" Trish asked.

He couldn't answer so he did what he always did: looked away from her and shrugged and murmured something about being fine, just fine.

In mid-September, Louis arrived with Sophie and Meg. It had taken them a couple of hours to get there from Kaatza, along the winding remains of the old highways, narrow and rough but passable as they hadn't been even two years before.

"It's good to see you, Soph," Kit told her as he helped her out of the jeep, hugged her, and realized how much she had changed in the two years since their last visit. Her bony arm clung to his shoulder, her frizzy hair thin, streaks of pink scalp showing. She muttered something like "yes" and climbed — slowly, carefully — up the single step to the porch, leaning hard on his shoulder. Then there was the chaos of getting Sophie settled in bed, Meg propped up beside her, wheezing and pale from the journey. The two looked so fragile that Kit had to turn away as Trish brought tea and kept away the visitors who wanted to see Sophie, and tell her things: about the Canadians, about the cathedral, about their plans. Everyone knew Sophie. Everyone wanted to touch her hand, share a smile. When he'd lived out at Kaatza she had been a giant in his mind, the tallest woman he'd ever seen, the strongest, out-working him in the garden, up at dawn, and falling into bed with the last light of the sun.

Outside, Louis told Kit about the trip: how easy the route had become, how they'd followed new maps derived from live satellite feeds, how you could see — in a single image — the valley and the coast, how small they were, how close to the mainland. Here Louis pulled out one of the new tablets the Canadians had brought, to show him the whole South Island as seen from Chandra, the new space station, larger even than Tiangong. Fifty people up there, planning new missions to Mars, to see what had become of the settlements. Looking at the image for a long moment, and seeing yes — there is the village, and that must be the Cathedral, and there are the golden savannas all around the bay — Kit nodded, blinking away his vertigo. He asked, "you wanted to see how things are going?"

Together they walked through the nursery and the avenues of aurum that surrounded the Cathedral, roots sunk deep in the earth for kilometers around, so floods and windstorms might break branches, but never uproot the whole tree. On the beach, the Canadians were swimming, or sprawled in the evening sunlight, listening to some music from the tiny speakers they always carried with them. Louis stared at them with such steady longing Kit wanted to cover his eyes and send him back into the woods, which were — despite a thousand risks — safer than anything the Canadians could offer.

"Meg's worse. So is Soph," Louis said.

Kit nodded. Meg had been down from Kaatza the previous August, and a week when the thermometer had showed 47°C on the hillside. The afternoon so oppressive that all movement felt like a violation of the sky's injunction to absolute stillness. Stuck in the house with Trish, Meg was restless, in tears, near panic as each breath came harder and harder. Kit had walked back home to check on them, and hadn't thought about it, just picked Meg up and carried her down to the water, to immerse her, squalling, in the salt. It had not cooled her as much as he had hoped, and not for the first time a terrible rage rose in his throat at the billions of people who had lived strange, glorious lives spanning continents and planets, and abandoned him here with a little girl he couldn't help.

Louis asked, "Did they bring meds?"

"Yeah. The medic will take a look at her tomorrow." This conversation was, in fact, one of the first things he'd done after meeting Khush: what had they brought? What could they afford to share or trade?

The next morning, Kit was up before the first cry of the gulls, when the window was still dark and the front room full of quietly breathing bodies. Trish with Meg cuddled against her ribs, Louis curled up on his side as he used to do when he was a little boy asleep on the gravel near the beach fire, refusing to go in, but too tired to keep his eyes open.

Unable to sleep, he crept out from among them and found his boots on the front porch. By the time he heard birds and the air had brightened above Saltspring Island, Kit was on the porch, sowing winter cabbage in sand and compost, thinking about how he'd slip out to the Cathedral while he could —

"— Kit?" An early-morning voice from the doorway.

"Soph!" he said. "Why are you even up?"

She held out her arm. "Old women never sleep. Come on, help me down the steps. I want to see the rest of the sunrise." she said, looking down to the longhouse on the beach. "What about the invasion?"

"They're kids," Kit said. "So young."

She snorted, affectionate and a little derisive. The snort was so much like herself, and so unlike the frail woman he had seen the night before, he said, "I'm glad you came down."

"I didn't want to. What are they like?"

"Nice."

Sophie inspected the newly sown cabbages, then picked up his watering can and doused the corners he'd missed.

"You've put in another potato field, Trish said."

Relieved to talk about anything but the invasion, he went on at length about the south-facing location, the amendments they'd made, the sand they'd carted in from an old quarry up the hill. His ideas for rotation. The possibility of cereal grains.

"Do you need a whole acre?"

"Maybe not, but we're sending potatoes and apples down-island these days, and they're growing some winter wheat over in Saanich. Enough to trade. We're looking at more orchards, too."

"I'd worry about water. And then salination. Is it high enough?"

"Maybe, but who knows. We're thinking canals down to the estuary, where the old farms were. Be a big project."

"You like big projects. The cathedral."

He nodded again.

"Mason would have liked it."

The thought of Mason's approval stopped Kit. "You remember how he used to fill up that backpack with spruce seedlings and hike out into the valleys? Do you think any of them survived?"

"Some of them. Maybe."

Kit wanted to ask her how she had slept through all the dark days of decline, when she and Jake held by their fingertips against forest fires and floods, how they had fought the slow erosion of topsoil for years, filling sandbags made from whatever they could find: old curtains from an abandoned house or the beach towels from vacations no one took anymore. He wanted to say, Soph tell the truth: through it all your brain was screaming and your heart was screaming and you hung on, sure, but didn't you wonder if any of it made a difference?

When he looked up at her, Soph's eyes were sharp and clear. The disoriented old woman of the previous night was entirely gone, replaced by this familiar figure: Soph, a woman who saw everything, even when she chose not to speak.

"Are you sleeping?"

Kit shrugged and asked, "Have you been talking to Trish?"

"You're not sleeping."

"You want to come up and see it? You can ride in the cart."

He pushed her to top of the hill, where the Cathedral glowed with early sunshine, so bright Kit blinked and shaded his eyes. Soph broke the silence. "I remember following a runner once from an aurum sapling out by the lake. We dug a few hundred meters. It was still going. No other tree in sight. I wonder how big they are? Mason guessed that all the aurum were one tree. A clonal colony, like aspen, a huge organism. They inosculate so easily, growing apart and together again. How do you propagate?

"Cuttings. Sarwan figures they're sterile."

"Clones then. That's probably good. The whole island is going to be gold, eventually. And not just one species. Just one tree."

Kit shivered. "Where did it come from?"

"Some experiment. Maybe a lucky adaptation. Maybe the Canadians have some record of what was going on in forestry at SFU or UBC or U-Dub. I heard a story once," she said abruptly, and silence fell, Kit waiting because he understood she had marked the beginning of something important, that couldn't be rushed.

"I heard a story once," she repeated, her voice slower now. "That it's arbutus roots that hold the world together. We need that tap root. You know how deep the old trees could go. And these aurum — they go farther than that."

"A tap root. Where'd you hear that?"

"I can't remember. Maybe I read it in a book, or Jake told me. It's probably the kind of story they used to sell real estate, imaginary Indian legends to make a place seem more interesting. But I still think about it and wonder where those came from."

Kit wanted to tell her something important, maybe give her something precious so she could hold it in those strong fingers as she had done with babies and the tender roots of trees and the hands of the dying and the chicks she raised out at the lake and the seeds she collected. Instead, he rested a light hand on her shoulder and asked, "Are you cold?"

She touched the walls of the Cathedral, "You've made something, kid," she said.

That afternoon a very young woman from Canada listened to Meg's chest and tested her blood oxygen with a finger oximeter. A few questions: When had she started wheezing? What triggered it? Did anyone else in the family have problems breathing?

"It's probably asthma. That's an autoimmune disorder," the young woman began. "Which means it's her own body attacking —"

"— We know that," Trish said. "What can we do about it?"

"I mean there are a ton of therapies we do back home. I can probably help a bit though."

Then a puff from a plastic tube, and a pill. In half an hour Meg's breathing was deep and regular and the tight lines around her mouth loosened into a smile. She coughed up a throatful of phlegm. Then she was hungry. She wanted to go down to the beach. She wanted to pet Grandma's cat. She wanted to run.

That night, the Corps talked about Arctic re-settlement and new uranium exploration in what had been the Northwest Territories. Kit knew, then, that other groups of joyful young people had been sent there, as well, to whoever was left on the land. Maybe they'd gone east, too: PEI, Newfoundland. Images of tundra hung in the smoke of their nighttime fire, three dimensional ghosts from these tiny projectors they'd set up to show drone footage of old mines, radomes leftover from another century, then a queasily accelerating image of the surviving caribou running breakneck. Louis watched with an intensity that filled Kit with fear, like he could see the world blooming in Louis's eyes, how he was already half gone to the mainland, where who knew how far he'd travel. Kit held Trish's hand so tightly she nudged him until he loosened his grip. They sat with their backs against the logs, Meg asleep between them, her breath coming easily for the first time that Kit could remember.

The Canadians liked to play music and show them movies. They also liked to record: films and photographs on their ubiquitous tablets, but also interviews for some big project they talked about back home that the historians were doing at the country's surviving university humanities department. Trish was good at it, remembering her parents, her cousins, including dates and years. She talked about Benno and the burn, about the cottage she and Kit had built together on the remains of some old cul-de-sac. Sarwan talked about the number of seedlings he produced each year, and how he'd learned to use the CRISPR-6 from an old man who'd gone to university a million years before. Sophie shared Nepenthe until the interviewer girl chilled, then they talked about the market garden, more than a century old, the work of Jake's grandmother who'd homesteaded in the 1970s. How it had sustained them through the fiery decades, how they'd expanded it along the lake, building the soil a few centimeters a year. How they'd learned to tend forest gardens, eating crab apples and hazelnuts and salal berries during the long, rainy winters.

Kit hung around to listen, especially when she got to the stories about Jake and Mason: The time they poached an old growth spruce to make a violin. The time Jake stayed up for forty-eight hours keeping the flooding river out of town, how he came home and just managed to get through the door and onto the mat in the entrance hall before he lost consciousness. That happened surprisingly often, where Soph'd wake up in the morning and find him asleep on the floor, muddy boots still on his feet. That was Jake, though — a sucker for work. A thin, wiry frame, arms roped with muscle, made to hold on all night, all day.

From there to Benno, Trish and Soph swapping stories about his curiosity, his recklessness, crossing the Salish in a kayak just to see what was happening in Vancouver. The time he walked the valley's coastline collecting books from abandoned houses, dragging them in a trailer along the old highway, and carrying them across each washout on his back. Soph laughing to tell how Benno arrived at Kaatza looking like a madman, his long black hair full of burrs and sticks and mud, raving about the books he'd found.

"Where did the books come from?" the Canadian asked.

"They came up island when they dissolved the library at UVic, sixty years ago maybe? Benno's granddad started collecting them, and he just kept it up. A lot of them are out at Kaatza now. That's all Benno's doing. And it's not just practical stuff. He liked poetry when he could find it."

After that Soph was pretty tired, so she sat back, listening while Meg sang a skipping rhyme:

She is brave and she is pretty
she sings songs from the golden city
She eats salmon, she drinks beer
She'll come back to us next year.
She gets lost, she gets found
how many years til she comes round?
(Doubletime) 1! 2! 3! 4! 5!

When Kit's turn came he tried to describe what he did, but the story receded further from his tongue with each stuttered beginning, until he lapsed into silence, and the girl (sober again) nudged him with questions.

"Where did you grow up?" she asked. "Tell me about your mom and dad."

He shook his head. "I don't —"

"We can do it later if you —"

"— naw. I don't. Naw."

And thank God there was already someone new to take his place, a chatty old aunty from town, eager to talk about the dead, and describe in detail the location of long-demolished buildings, the genealogies of second cousins, their rivalries and entanglements. Good weddings. Terrible weddings.

A glance at Trish, then Kit walked up the hill toward the cathedral, his eyes fixed on its highest limbs, stretching toward one another, but not yet meeting in the roof he had imagined. He thought, This is all I have to say. These slender interlocking trunks, these branches and sheltering leaves, this vision of a human life that was part of all the teeming kingdoms below ground and in the sky above. A world full of birds and honey-bees, so deeply rooted it might — if they were brave and clever and lucky — survive what would come next. If the Canadian girl wanted to know anything about the village and its history, she should look up the hill toward the cathedral, and record the sounds of wind in its branches, or see the dawn from its cloister. She should walk along the shore and let that be Kit's statement to all the historians that might come after.

If it wasn't for Trish, for the discovery of a hillside meadow, for camas and a controlled burn and Garry oak trees planted by some earlier arborist. If it wasn't for a bench not built but grown out of the branches of a tree. If it wasn't for Benno and Mason and Sophie and Jake. If it wasn't for Louis and Meg and Sarwan. If it wasn't for genetic techs and fisher-men, for forest gardens and potato fields and chickens and dairy cattle, and rabbits on the traplines, for black-tail deer and blackberries and ocean gardens along the shore where the oysters and mussels sometimes survived the heat of Salish summers. If it wasn't for old books, their covers torn away, and recovered aluminum and old cinder blocks and cannibalized electronics and many-times-mended solar cells. If it wasn't for Chinook in the Cowichan River, swimming upstream along a riverbed cut through the parking lot of the old shopping mall. If it wasn't for Jake stretched out flat in the front hall of the house on Kaatza, sleeping off twenty hours of work on the firebreak, or Mason lifting a seedling spruce from the earth in which it had sprouted, and carrying it into the mountains.

By late afternoon on the day of the party, you could smell salmon and lamb all the way up to the nurseries, a heavy fatty smoke brilliant with aromatics: dill and garlic, cedar planks, brightly acidic blackberries and bitter cherries, wakame and kelp. Fragrant herbs too, mint and cilantro and parsley. Somewhere, he knew, there were rosewater syllabubs, garnished with late strawberries. He'd eat as many of them as Trish would let him, which wasn't many according to her rules: cream upset his stomach, and hosts should hold back.

He was telling Khush something important, about living enclosures for cattle and sheep. Khush wasn't listening.

"Uh huh," he said. His eyes flicked down toward the beach.

"We need more — Christ. Okay. Come on. Let's go."

"Are we finished?"

He looked so damned hopeful. "Sure," Kit said.

The path they took back to the beach wound between rows of fruit trees. It smelled like grass and ripening apples, like salt. As they got closer to the beach, and could hear the talk, the laughter, Khush sped up.

Meg ran over as they joined the crowd.

"I have a secret, Grandpa," she said. "Guess!"

She held out her two closed fists and Kit bent to examine them, then — slowly, thoughtfully — he tapped her left fist. It was always the left fist with Meg. She giggled. Inside, a blackberry. It was the last of many, judging by the stains on her fingers and around her mouth.

He ate it. "That," he said, "is the best blackberry I have ever tasted, Meg. Thank you."

People had been coming for days, down the island by boat and on foot, or in wagons along the old highways, following those new satellite maps to the Canadians, who welcomed them all cheerfully, taking pictures and searching databases for the names of the long-lost, the ones who left fifty or sixty years before, but were nevertheless remembered in family legend.

He'd never seen the village this crowded, nor felt so uncomfortable. He'd seen pictures of groups far larger, and knew that there were more people than this on the island, but he still held tight to Trish's hand, while Meg's eyes grew larger with each new arrival.

"Hundreds and hundreds and hundreds," Meg whispered. "Is this all the people in the world? Is this Wellington?" Wellington was where the cartoons came from.

Trish answered, "No, honey. Just a few of them."

After dinner the crowd walked slowly up the hill to the cathedral. Inside, Kit and Trish found a corner near the vestibule at the side, leaving the seats open for Sophie, and the elderly Cathedralists like Sarwan, and visitors from up and down the valley. As he watched people gather, Kit held one of the branches, running his hand across the healthy scar that had formed where it intersected with its companion, no sign of infection and strong enough to support his weight when he climbed up the wall. He knew this arch so well, had seen it first in architectural diagrams, had calculated its proportions, then bound them into its trunk, to entwine, here, through a scar in its skin, with another branch, to form a curve that rose to its apex above their heads. Fifteen years ago he had shaped that archway, and here it remained, stronger with every season, the scars of its inosculation faded further into its golden skin as its branches reached for what would be the Cathedral's crown.

When Louis brought Soph in, Kit first smiled, then saw that she had again changed into the old woman she had been on her arrival, her face blank and internal. All around her people waved and smiled and sang out, *Sophie! Sophie!* It was too noisy, too late, the evening too hot for her. She should be somewhere quiet and safe. He thought, I'll take her down to the water where it's quiet. Forget about all this —

Here he felt Trish's hand first on his elbow, then encircling his fingers.

"Is she okay?" he asked. "She looks ..."

"I know. She wants to be here. This morning she said she remembers it. She didn't at first, and she couldn't understand what I was talking about, when I told her about Belinda and Nepenthe. Then this morning she said yes, I remember."

The chattering stilled. Somewhere a girl was still giggling alongside the cracked rumble of a boy's voice. Belinda's son walked through the crowd to the stone dais at its center, where he set up his keyboard under the unobtrusive spotlights and cameras and mics the Canadians had clipped to the branches overhead. The air smelled of cooking fires and green leaves and sweat and warm earth and skin and Trish.

Belinda joined the young man. The violin glowed in her arms, its spruce face so finely worked, so well loved, it seemed to gather light to it. Applause and more conversation as the two waited for the crowd to exhaust its joy and fall silent again.

Kit tried to contain his habitual and long-suppressed grief: for his mother and father, who died young in the years after the Desettlement. For Meg, with black hair like Trish's and brown eyes and a huge laugh ready and wild in her mouth when the dog caught a ball or the cat flopped onto his back for belly rubs. Meg, for whom Trish camped two days outside the clinic in Duncan, waiting for the visiting doctor to confirm the diagnosis they already suspected. Meg, who spent August heatwaves sleeping upright because when she lay down her lungs felt too big for her chest.

His heart, too, was tight in his chest as he looked through the walls to the water below. Each September seemed warmer than the one before, dryer, the fire season lengthening into October, November. No matter how small their lives had become, no matter how light their step or how many tons of carbon the Canadians sequestered, the sea was still rising. Khush had shown him pictures of Greenland's ice melting down the glacial mountainsides to stain the salt arctic waters green, while far to the south whole ice sheets still fell into the Ross Sea. It had happened and it was happening and it would happen. Even if they retook Victoria's suburbs and turned them all to farmland and savanna. Even if carbon-hungry aurum overgrew the hillsides in root-structures so large, no one was sure of their scale. Even if the whole island was inhabited by a single tree, turning it to gold and summiting Mount Newton, to reach its branches high above the encroaching waters. To which they could tether themselves, as people had in another age of rising waters.

He couldn't breathe. The young man began to play an old-fashioned piece that made the little girls get up and hold hands, dancing in a circle before him. Meg left them to join in, no wheezing as she laughed along with the playful melody. When he finished, the girls clapped and the cathedral settled again into rustling quiet, children leaned against their parents' knees.

He couldn't breathe. The beach would be gone in Meg's lifetime — how long would that pill work? How long before a winter infection carried her away? — and the remaining Douglas firs would go, their range curtailed to the south, moving north with the temperate weather. And Louis would be gone with the Canadians to who knew where, and Soph was dying and maybe Sarwan would go and what would they do without the last of the old folks?

Meg had returned from her dance to sit on the ground beside him, her arm wrapped around his knee as another playful piano melody modulated into something somber and beautiful. Her face transfixed by music she had never heard before. And though Soph's eyes were full of tears, she was still with them. And though Louis sat with the Canadians, he had not yet disappeared into the mainland. As though she knew — of course she knew, how could she not? — Trish slid her fingers between Kit's, and he felt the rough, warm skin of her palm pressed tight against his, her lips moving in a whisper so quiet he leaned down to catch her words. Breathe, she was saying. Breathe.

He breathed in and he breathed out and he reached up into the walls of the cathedral to grip a golden branch.

It is 18 September 2100 and the full moon rises over Cowichan Bay and a half-grown cathedral, still a century away from its most perfect form. Above the Earth, on Chandra, the new International Space Station, Lin awakens on the first day of their expedition and observes the moon and laughs to see its glorious rising over the blue rim of the Earth. In a pond in Texas a small brown frog dies in the throat of a Great Blue Heron, the last, unnamed scion of its species. A lightning strike in San Diego sparks a wildfire that will wipe out an experimental farm and the two hundred people who work it. In a cabin on Great Slave Lake a little girl hears the high lonesome howl of wolves and shivers in pleasure and fear, hiding deeper under the covers of her bed. A young woman in Seattle also shivers, the first sign of a new variant of some old virus. Outside Sitka, a yearling spruce tree with golden needles rises in the shadow of its green-branched mother, sharing carbon and nitrogen along the mycorrhizal networks that connect them. A glass float from a nineteenth-century Japanese fisherman finally drifts ashore at Ucluelet after more than two centuries at sea. On the bank of a river in SoWestO, overtaken by moonlight, Khush's brother kisses another boy for the first time and falls instantly and absolutely in love, a moment so brilliant it will illuminate the rest of his life. On the shore of Cowichan Bay, Sophie listens to the wind disturbing the branches of a beautiful and unnatural

Acknowledgments

Thanks go to Neil Clarke, who gave "An Important Failure" space in *Clarkesworld*, and then to Selena Middleton, who encouraged the story to grow into something new. Thank you, also, to David Bodaly, Snuneymuxw Knowledge Keeper, and to Tegan Moore, Sarah Ervine, Sean Henry, Dave Hickey, and Jeff Strain. Finally, I am grateful to my family, living and dead: Sharron and David, "Cam" Campbell, Paulette Fitzgerald, Ian Campbell, Don and David Bourne.

The Ontario Arts Council supported this project with a generous grant, for which I am grateful.

About the Author

Rebecca Campbell is a Canadian writer of weird stories and climate change fiction. Her work has appeared in many magazines and anthologies, including *The Magazine of Fantasy and Science Fiction*, *Clarkesworld*, and *Interzone*. She won the Sunburst award for short fiction in 2020 for "The Fourth Trimester is the Strangest" and the Theodore Sturgeon Memorial Award in 2021 for "An Important Failure." NeWest Press published her first novel, *The Paradise Engine*, in 2013. You can find her online at whereishere.ca.

If you loved this book you might also like *Night Roll* by Michael J. DeLuca

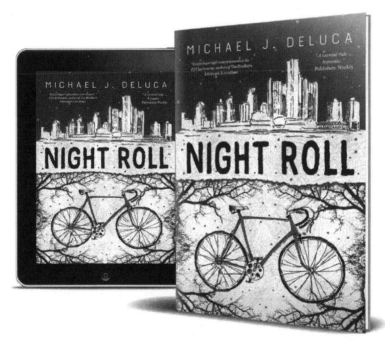

A finalist for the prestigious IAFA William L. Crawford Fantasy Award, *Night Roll* is the story of a new mother finding community and unexpectedly rebellious magic in a resurgent climate-changed Detroit. Find *Night Roll* wherever books are sold. Digital books are always on sale at www.stelliform.press.

STELLIFORM PRESS

**Earth-focused fiction. Stellar stories.
Stelliform.press.**

Stelliform Press is shaping conversations about
our climate changed world and our place within
it. We invite you to join the conversation by
leaving a comment or review on your favorite
social media platform. Find us on the web at
www.stelliform.press and on Twitter, Instagram
and Facebook @StelliformPress.